William O. Stoddard

With the Black Prince

William O. Stoddard

With the Black Prince

ISBN/EAN: 9783337172015

Printed in Europe, USA, Canada, Australia, Japan

Cover: Foto ©Andreas Hilbeck / pixelio.de

More available books at **www.hansebooks.com**

Firm as a rock stood the young warrior.

(See page 18.)

WITH THE BLACK PRINCE

BY

WILLIAM O. STODDARD

AUTHOR OF
CROWDED OUT O' CROFIELD, THE RED PATRIOT,
SUCCESS AGAINST ODDS, ETC.

ILLUSTRATED

NEW YORK
D. APPLETON AND COMPANY
1898

CONTENTS.

v

LIST OF ILLUSTRATIONS.

WITH THE BLACK PRINCE.

CHAPTER I.

THERE came a sudden sound, breaking the shadowy silence of Longwood forest.

Crash followed crash, at short intervals, with the snapping of dry twigs and bush branches, and then came ringing, clear and sweet, three notes of a hunting horn.

Out into an open glade, where the sunlight fell upon the long, green grass of midsummer, there bounded a splendid stag—a stag royal, a stag of ten—fit to be the antlered monarch of the king's deer in Longwood.

Three leaps, and then the beautiful animal stood still; but as he turned, panting, and lowered his horns, it could be seen that he was wounded. The feather of an arrow in his flank told how deeply the shaft was driven.

He was at bay now, and splendid was his courage as he stood to battle with his pursuers.

1

Again, and nearer, nearer, sounded the horn;
for the hunters were coming.

Out through the leafy barrier of the bushes at
the edge of the glade bounded three eager deer-
hounds, one after another. Large dogs they were,
brown-haired, lop-eared. Their baying had chimed
in with the music of the horn. Better for them it
were if one of the huntsmen had been there to
hold them from their haste; for there is danger
for any who rush rashly in upon a stag at bay.

Loud voices and the thud of galloping hoofs
told that the hunters were close at hand; but they
were too late in arriving. The foremost hound
dashed fiercely on, his white teeth showing, and
his eyes flashing with green light; but the ten-
tined antlers passed under him and were lifted
swiftly.

Away the hound was hurled, pierced fatally,
and then a sudden side stroke disabled the second
of the four-footed assailants. The third paused,
lifting a forefoot doubtfully as he glanced from
one to the other of his unlucky companions. A
whizzing shaft passed over his head, and a cloth-
yard arrow sped to its mark, inside the shoulder of
the deer. The spreading antlers plowed the sod
for a moment, and then all was over. A tall, pow-
erful-looking man, who came riding up, sprang
from his horse, and stood by the wounded dogs,
exclaiming:

"These short-legged galloways have cost us two hounds! We had better stalk a deer than run him, unless we have swifter steeds."

"Stalking must serve our turn, now the dogs are gone," growled a shorter man who had come up and now stood beside him. "I would the legs of our nags had been longer!"

They were rough-looking men, and they spoke in the burred Saxon-English of Warwickshire five hundred years ago. It was another tongue from any now spoken in England.

The galloways, of whose legs they had complained, were the undersized and shaggy-maned horses they had ridden in that hunt. Such were plentiful then, but none other could be had save by those who could pay large prices.

"Fools are we," remarked another man. "And mayhap the horn blast has gone to the wrong ears with token of our doings. That was thy blowing, Guy the Bow."

"And what care we?" responded the tall hunter. "'Tis long since there hath been a royal keeper in any wood of Arden Forest. Earl Warwick himself never hunteth as far to the north as this. There's no harm in a horn, and I like well the sound, and the baying o' the dogs. We'll not again hear either very soon."

Others had now come up, but they said little. They lifted their game to the back of one of the galloways. The arrows were carefully extracted, cleaned, and restored to the quivers of their own-ers. The men were all stalwart fellows, and the bows they carried were tremendous weapons. When unstrung, such a bow would rest upon a man's foot and touch his nose, and only a strong and practiced arm could bend one. Besides the bows, they carried short, two-edged swords hang-ing at their belts, in which were also stuck broad-bladed knives or daggers. They wore no armor except light headpieces of steel, and their garments appeared to be made of leather. The body coats were like leather blouses, soiled and worn. They wore leggings of deerskin, but several were bare-footed.

A brave-looking dozen were these hunters of Longwood. Their faces were not evil, and their talk was that of kindly men fond of adventure and of sport, but caring little whose deer they were taking.

The carcass of the stag had been bound to one of the horses, and the hunters were mounting, when a loud shout came from under the nearest oaks:

"Ho, there! Halt! What do ye, killing the king's deer?"

"Stand for your lives, men!" exclaimed Guy the Bow. "I'll not be taken!"

"Nor I!" roared a burly hunter at his side;

"but—it's young Neville of Wartmont. I could not strike him."

Only five men came riding out from under the trees, but they were all well mounted, and were better armed than were the hunters. Every man of them wore linked mail, with shield and lance and sword, while at every saddlebow hung a mace or battleaxe. Their helmets were open in front, and the face of the foremost rider was that of a beardless boy. It was a very resolute face, how-ever, and he raised his hand as he again demanded:

"In the king's name, what do ye?"

"We be free men," said Guy sturdily. "Lit-tle reason hath thy father's son to question our acts."

"Why not?" came back. "Yonder stag is a death-warrant for every man of you!"

"Not so," exclaimed the burly hunter. "I am Ben o' Coventry, and we all stand by Guy the Bow. Will thy mail shirt keep out a cloth-yard shaft, Richard Neville of Wartmont?"

An arrow was on every bowstring at that mo-ment; but Guy the Bow spoke again.

"Thou art a boy, Richard Neville," he said. "I will tell thee somewhat thou shouldst know. Thou hast only the ruins of thy tower to dwell in; but when Earl Mortimer claimed thy father's barony, and sent his men to put his seneschal in holding, the yeomen of Wartmont and Longwood,

and more from further on in Arden, stood by the
Neville. The Mortimer raided our holdings, burning house and barn. He lost his head years on,
and thy uncle is Earl of Warwick; but the bowmen of these parts had become used to taking Earl
Mortimer's deer."

"They are the king's deer now," said Richard.
"Ye know that well."

"They bear no mark," grumbled Ben, lowering
his bow. "We'll call that stag for Mortimer, this
day, in spite of the Neville. Take us not. Go
back to your tower."

"My young lord," was spoken in a low voice
from among the men in mail behind him, "let them
alone. They are thine own men. It's only a deer
more or less. There are foes enough. Hark to
Ben once more."

"I heard thee, sir," said Ben gratefully. "He
might do well to heed thy saying; but let him
now hear what Guy may tell him."

"My young Lord of Wartmont," said Guy, "I
had verily thought to go and see thee this day.
Knowest thou not that Clod of Lee, the Club of
Devon, hath been heard from this side the Avon?
He was one of Mortimer's men, and he hateth thee
and thine. He is a wolf's head, by all law. He
and his outlaws would find at Wartmont much that
such as they would seek. Go in haste and hold
thy tower against them, if thou canst, and bother

not thyself with a free hunt and a nag-load of
venison."

"Thou art no king's forester," added Ben of
Coventry. "These are times when a man may let
well enough alone."

"He speaketh truly," whispered Richard's
mailed adviser. "Ride we to the castle as fast as
we may. Thy mother——"

"Not a dozen swordsmen are at the Mount!"
exclaimed Richard. "My mother is unprotected!
Guy the Bow, I thank thee for thy warning.
What care I for a few deer? Only, watch thou
and thy men; for the earl sendeth soon to put this
part of the shire under close forest law. None
may escape if work like this go on then."

"Thou art right, my young lord," responded
Guy; "but the yeomen of Longwood have no fel-
lowship with the wolves of Devon and Cornwall.
It is said, too, that there be savage Welsh among
these outlaws that spare neither woman nor child.
Ride thou with speed, and God be with thee!
Well for thee that they are not bowmen, like thy
neighbors."

"Haste, my lord!" cried another of Richard's
men. "There are many women and there are children at the tower."

"On! on!" shouted Richard; but his face
was white, as he wheeled his horse southward.

Very terrible was the name which had been

won by some of the robber bands of England.
They had been more numerous during the reign of
Edward the Second. His son, Edward the Third,
was only fourteen years of age when he was
crowned, and it was several years more before he
really became king. Ever since then he had
striven with only moderate success to restore order
throughout his realm. Several notable bodies of
savage marauders were still to be heard from only
too frequently, while in many districts the yeomen
paid as little attention to the forest laws as if they
had been Robin Hood's merry men of Sherwood.
This was not the case upon the lands of the great
barons, but only where there was no armed force at
hand to protect the game. The poachers were all
the safer everywhere because of the strong popular feeling in their favor, and because any informer
who should give the life of a man for that of a
deer might thenceforth be careful how he ventured
far into the woods. He was a mark for an arrow
from a bush, and not many cared to risk the vengeance of the woodsmen.

On rode the young Neville and his four men-at-
arms; but hardly had they disappeared among the
forest glades before Ben of Coventry turned upon
his galloway to ask:

"Guy the Bow, what thinkest thou? The
Wartmont boy spoke not unkindly. There be
kith and kin of the forest men at the tower.

What if the Club of Lee should reach the moat
and find the gate open? 'Tis a careless time."

"Hang up the stag and follow!" at once
commanded Guy, captain of the hunt. "We
have taken three the day. There will be venison at every hearth. If only for his father's
sake——"

"We are not robbers, Guy the Bow," interrupted another of his followers. "We are true
men. 'Twill be a wolf hunt instead of a deer
hunt. I like it well."

They strung up the stag to a bough of a tree,
and then wheeled with a shout and galloped away
as merrily as if they had started another hart
royal.

Three long miles away, easterly from the glade
where the stag had fallen, the forest ended; and
beyond the scattered dignities of its mighty oaks
lay a wide reach of farm land. The fields were
small, except some that seemed set aside for pas-
tures and meadows. There were well-grown but
not very well-kept hedges. There were a few
farmhouses, with barns and ricks. Nearly in the
center rose a craggy hill, and at the foot of this
clustered a small hamlet. It was a sign of the
troubles that Edward the Third had striven to
quell that all along the outer border of the hamlet
ran the tattered remnants of what once had been a
strong line of palisades and a deep ditch.

2

The hill was the Wart Mount, and on its crest were massive walls with a high, square tower at one corner. Viewed from a distance, they seemed to be a baronial stronghold. On a nearer approach, however, it could be seen that the beauty and strength of Wartmont had been marred by fire, and that much of it needed rebuilding. Some repairs had been made on the tower itself. Its gateway, with moat and bridge, was in fair condition for defense. More than one road led across the open country toward the castle; but the highway was from the east, and travelers thereon were hidden from sight by the hill.

There was a great stir in the village, for a man came riding at full speed from one of the farmhouses, shouting loudly as he passed the old palisades:

"To the hill! To the castle! The wolves of Devon are nigh! They have wasted Black Tom's place, and have slain every soul!"

The warning had already traveled fast and far, and from each of the farmhouses loaded wains, droves of cattle, horses, sheep, were hurrying toward the hill. Women, with their children, came first, weeping and praying.

Far away, on the southerly horizon, arose a black cloud of smoke to tell of the end of Black Tom's wheatstacks and haystacks.

"Aye! aye!" mourned an old woman. "It's

gone wi' fire! Alas! And the good king is in
Flanders the day, and his people are harried as if
they had no king."

"It's like the old time," said another, "when
all the land was wasted. I mind the telling o'
what the Scots did for the north counties till the
king drave them across the border."

Well kept were the legends that were told
from one generation to another in the days when
there were no books or newspapers; and they were
now rehearsed rapidly, while the affrighted farm
people fled from their threatened homes, as their
ancestors had many a time been compelled to do.
Still they all seemed to have great faith in the
castle, and to believe that when once there they
would be safe.

The rider who brought the news did not pause
in the village, but rode on, and dismounted at the
bridge over the moat. Not stopping to hitch his
panting horse, he strode into the open portal, sending his loud message of evil omen through the corridor beyond. Voice after voice took up the cry
and carried it up through the tower and out into
the castle yard, till it seemed to find weird echoes
among the half-ruined walls. At no place were
these altogether broken down. There was no
breach in them. Large parts of the old structures
were still roofed over, and along the battlements
there quickly appeared the forms of old and young,

peering out eagerly to see whatever there might be to see upon the lowland.

There were very few men, apparently; but in the lower rooms of the tower there were quickly clanking sounds, as shields and weapons and armor were taken down from their places.

A large open area was included within the outer walls, and there was room for quadrupeds as well as for human beings. Still there was a promise of close crowding, if all the fugitives on the roads were to be provided for.

Gathered now in the village street was a motley crowd of men. They were by no means badly armed, but they seemed to have no commander, and their hurried councils were of all sorts. Most seemed to favor a general retreat to the castle, but against this course was urged the fact that the marauders had not yet arrived, nor had all the people from the farms.

"Men!" exclaimed a portly woman with a scythe in her strong hands, "could ye not meet them at the palisades? Bar the gap with a wain. There are bows and crossbows among ye. Fight them there!"

"We could never hold them back," came doubtfully from one of the men. "They'd find gaps enough. It's only a stone wall can stop them."

"They'll plunder the village," the woman said.

"Better that than the blood of us all," responded the man. "We are few. Would the young
lord were here with his men-at-arms !"

"He rode to the north the morn," she was told.
"Only four were with him. The rest are far away
with the earl. A summons came, telling that the
Scots were over the border."

"Could not the north counties care for themselves, without calling on the midlands?" grumbled the woman.

At that moment there came a terrified shriek
from the road-gap in the palisades. The last of
several wains was passing in, and all the street was
thronged with cattle.

"They come! They come!" screamed the
women by that wain. "Oh, that they gat so nigh,
and none to see ! It's over with us the day ! Yon
is the Club, and his men are many !"

Partly mounted, but some of them on foot, a
wild-looking throng of men came pouring across a
stubble-field from the southward. It seemed as if
they might be over a hundred strong. No marching order was observed. There was no uniformity
in their arms. At the head of them strode a huge,
black-haired, shaggy-bearded brute who bore a tremendous club of oak, bound at its heavier end with
a thick ring of iron. He laughed and shouted as
he came, as if with a savage pleasure over the wild
deeds he had done and the prospect before him.

"Short work!" he roared to those behind him. "Burn all ye can not take. And then for the hills o' Wales! But we'll harry as we go!"

Other things he said that sounded as if he had an especial grudge against the king and against all who, like the Nevilles, had been his strong personal adherents.

The castle gateway was thronged, so that getting in was slow, but the yard was already filling fast. So were the rooms of the tower, and such as remained of the ruined buildings. Everywhere were distress and terror, except upon one face just inside the portal.

Tall and stately was Maud Neville, the widowed lady of Wartmont Castle. Her hair was white, but she was as erect as a pine, and all who looked into her resolute face might well have taken courage. Some seemed to do so, and around her gathered a score of stalwart retainers, with shields, axes, and swords. Some who had bows were bidden to man the loopholes on the second floor, and bide their time. Here, at least, if not in the village, there was a captain, and she was obeyed.

"Men," she said, "you know well what wolves these are. If they force their way into the keep, not one of us will be left to tell the tale."

A chorus of loyal voices answered her, and the men gripped their weapons.

So was it on that side of the hill; but on the

other, toward the east, the highway presented
another picture. Whether they were friends or
foemen, there was none to tell; but they were a
warlike band of horsemen. They were not
mounted upon low-built galloways, but upon steeds
of size and strength. The horsemen themselves
wore mail and carried lances, and several of them
had vizored helmets. They were ten in number,
riding two abreast, and one of the foremost pair
carried a kind of standard—a flag upon a long,
slender staff. It was a broad, square piece of blue
silk bunting, embroidered with heraldic devices
that required a skilled reader to interpret them.

Strangely enough, according to the ideas and
customs of the times, the rabble that followed
Clod the Club had also a banner. It was a somewhat tattered affair; but it must once have been
handsome. Its field was broad and white, and
any eyes could see that its dimmed, worn blazon
had been intended for three dragons. Perhaps the
robber chief had reasons of his own for marching
with a flag which must have been found in Wales.
It may have aided him in keeping at his command
some men who retained the old fierce hatred of
the Welsh for the kings of England.

He and his savages had now reached the palisades. The village men retreated slowly up the
street, while the remainder of those who could not
fight passed across the drawbridge and entered the

castle gate. More than one sturdy woman, however, had picked up a pike or an axe or a fork, and
stood among her kindred and her neighbors.

Not all the cattle nor all the wains could be
cared for ; and a shout from the portal summoned
the villagers to make more haste, that the gate
might be closed behind them. Part of them had
been too brave and part too irresolute, and there
was no soldiership in their manner of obeying.
They were, indeed, almost afraid to turn their
backs, for arrows were flying now.

Well it was for them that there seemed to be
so few good archers among the outlaws; for down
went man after man, in spite of shields or of such
armor as they had. Better shooting was done by
the men of Wartmont themselves, and the archers
in the tower were also plying their bows. It was
this that made the Club of Devon shout to his
wolves to charge, for the shafts were doing deadly
work.

With loud yells, on they rushed; and further
retreat was impossible. The foremost fighters on
each side closed in a desperate strife, and the
Wartmont farmers showed both skill and strength.
Half of them carried battle-axes or poleaxes, and
they plied them for their lives. Had it not been
for Clod himself, the rush might even have been
checked; but nothing could stand before him.
He fought like a wild beast, striking down foemen

right and left, and making a pathway for his followers.

Victory for the outlaws would have been
shortly gained but for the help that came to the
villagers.

"Onward, my men!" shouted Lady Maud, as
she sprang across the narrow bridge. "Follow
me! Save your kith and kin!"

"We will die with you!" cried out her retainers
as they pushed forward, while the archers in the
tower hurried down to join them.

Still they were too few; and the white head of
the brave woman was quickly the center of a surging mass, her entire force being almost surrounded
by the horde of robbers.

No shout came up the road. There was no
sound but the rapid thud of horses' feet; but suddenly five good lances charged furiously in among
the wolves. The foremost horseman went clean
through them, but his horse sank, groaning, as a
Welsh pike stabbed him, and his rider barely
gained his feet as the horse went down. Sword
in hand, then, he turned to face his foes, but he
spoke not to them.

"Mother!" he shouted, "I am here!"

"Thank God for thee, my son!" responded
the brave woman. "Thou art but just in time!"

Dire had been her peril, at that moment, but
Richard's presence gave courage to the defenders,

while his charge had staggered the outlaws. He was more than a match, with three of his dismounted men-at-arms at his side, for the foes immediately in front of them. His fourth follower lay several yards away, with his steel cap beaten in by a blow of the terrible club.

"Hah! hah! hah!" yelled Clod as he turned from that victim to press his way toward young Neville. "Down with him! Out of my path! Give the youngster to me!"

"Face him, my son!" said Lady Maud, "and Heaven's aid be with thee! Oh, for some o' the good king's men!"

"I have thee!" roared Clod, swinging high his club and preparing for a deadly blow.

Firm as a rock stood the young warrior, raising his shield to parry.

Down came the club, but forward flashed the sword with an under-thrust.

"O my son!" burst from the lips of the Lady of Wartmont. "My son hath fallen! Stand firm, men!"

Fallen, indeed, but so had Clod the Club, pierced through by the sword-thrust; and a fierce yell burst from his followers as they sprang forward to avenge him. They had been faring badly, but they were many and they were desperate. They might even yet have broken through the men of the tower who had stepped in front of Richard while his mother knelt to lift him, but for another turn in the strange fortunes of the day.

There was no warning, and all were too intent on the fray to note the arrival of newcomers; but now there came a sudden dropping of the outer men of the throng of robbers. Shaft after shaft, unerring, strongly driven, pierced them from back to breast.

"Shoot close!" shouted a voice. "Miss not. Steady, men! O Richard Neville of Wartmont, we are the killers of the king's deer!"

"Aye!" added Ben of Coventry. "We are with Guy the Bow, and 'tis a wolf-hunt!"

They were not many, but their archery was terrible. Fast twanged the bows, and fast the outlaws fell.

"Closer, men! Spare not any!" commanded Guy the Bow, and the line of galloways wheeled nearer.

It was too much. The remaining robbers would have fled if they could, but they were between two fires.

"O Richard!" murmured Lady Maud. "Thou art not dead?"

His fine dark eyes opened, just then, and a smile came faintly upon his lips as he replied:

"Only stunned, mother. The caitiff's club banged my shield down upon my head, but my

steel cap bore it well, else my neck were broken.
Did he go down ? "

"He lieth among the ruck," she said. "But oh,
thank God! The archers of Longwood have come!
The fight is won!"

It was won, indeed ; for neither the archers nor
the Wartmont men were showing any mercy to the
staggering, bewildered remnants of the outlaw
band which had been such a terror to the Welsh
border, and was to other counties almost as far
inland as was Warwick itself. Never more would
any peaceful hamlet or lonely tower be left in
ruins to tell of the ruthless barbarity of the wolves
of Devon.

Why they were so called, none knew ; but it
might be because that fair county had at one time
suffered most from their marauding, or because
fierce Clod the Club and some of his wild followers came from Lee on the Devon shore.

"Bloody work, my young Lord of Wartmont!
Bloody work, my lady!"

"Thank God for thee, Guy the Bow!" she responded. "Alas, my neighbors! But who cometh
there? My son, yonder is the flag of Cornwall,
and none may carry it but the prince himself. All
ye stand fast, but those who care for the hurt
ones."

These, indeed, were many, for the women and
children were pouring down from the castle.

With weeping and with wailing they were searching for their own among the dead and the wounded.
But even the mourners stood almost still for a
moment, as a knightly cavalcade came thundering
up the street.

The foremost horseman drew rein in front of
Lady Maud and her son, and the taller of them
demanded :

"O Lady Neville of Wartmont, what is this?
The prince rideth toward Warwick. I am Walter
de Maunay."

"His highness is most welcome," she said, with
calm dignity. "So art thou, Sir Walter. Around
thee are the dead wolves of Devon. Some of our
own people have fallen. Would thou wert here
an hour the sooner. God save the king!"

Rapid were the questions and the answers, but
the Black Prince himself, as he was called, left all
the talking to Sir Walter, while he dismounted to
study the meaning of the fray.

He had singularly keen, dark eyes, and they
flashed swiftly hither and thither, as if they were
seeking to know exactly how this small battle
had been fought and won.

"And this is the famous Clod the Club?" he
said. "By whose hand was this thrust?"

"'Twas young Lord Richard," answered Guy
the Bow. "Both went down, but the Neville was
little hurt. 'Twas bravely done !"

"Richard Neville," exclaimed the prince, "thou hast won honor in this! I would that I had slain him. Thou art a good sword. The king hath need of thee."

"He shall go with me," added Sir Walter admiringly, as he gazed down upon the massive form of the slain robber. "Madame, give the king thy son."

"Yea, and amen," she said. "He is the king's man. I would have him go. And I will bide at Warwick Castle until he cometh again. Speak thou, Richard!"

"I am the king's man," replied Richard, his face flushing. "O my mother, bid me go with the prince. I would be a knight, as was my father, and win my spurs before the king; but I fain would ask one favor of his grace."

"Ask on," said the prince. "'Twere hard to refuse thee after this gallant deed of arms."

"This work is less mine," said Richard, "than of Guy the Bow and my good forestmen. But I trow that some of them have found unlawful marks for other of their arrows. I ask for them the grace and pardon of the king."

"They have sinned against the king's deer," loudly laughed Sir Walter de Maunay. "There needeth no promise. Thou hast not heard of his royal proclamation. Free pardon hath he proclaimed to all such men as thine, if they will march with him against the King of France. 'Tis fair pay to every man, and the fortune of war beyond sea."

No voice responded for a moment as the archers studied one another's faces.

"Richard," said his mother, "speak thou to them. They wait for thee."

"O Guy the Bow," said Richard, "wilt thou come with me—thou and thy men?"

There was speech from man to man behind Guy; but it was Ben of Coventry who said:

"Tell thy prince, Guy the Bow, that two score and more of bows like thine will follow Richard Neville to fight for our good king."

To address the prince directly was more than Guy could do; but he spoke out right sturdily:

"My master of Wartmont, thou hearest the speech of Ben. 'Tis mine also. We take the pardon, and we will take the pay; and we will go as one band, with thee for our captain."

"Aye," said another archer, "with the young Neville and Guy the Bow."

"Ye shall be the Neville's own company," responded the prince. "I like it well. So will they do best service."

"Aye, 'tis the king's way also," added Sir Walter de Maunay; and then the Lady of Wartmont led the way into the castle.

Richard went not forthwith, but conferred with his archers.   He had care also for the injured and the dead, and to learn the harm done in the village and among the farms.

In a few minutes more, however, the banner of the prince was floating gayly from a corner of the tower, to tell to all who saw that the heir of the throne of England was under the Wartmont roof.

CHAPTER II.

THE MEN OF THE WOODS.

LACKING in many things, but not in stately hos-
pitality or in honest loyalty, was the welcome given
that night at Wartmont Castle to the heir of the
English throne and to his company.

Truth to tell, the fortunes of this branch of the
great house of Neville were not at their best. The
brave Sir Edward Neville had fallen in Flanders
fighting for the king. His widow and her only
son had found themselves possessed of much land,
but of little else. Too many acres of the domain
were either forest or hill, that paid neither tithe nor
rental. Not even Lady Maud's near kinship to the
Earl of Warwick was as yet of any avail, for these
were troublous times. Many a baron of high name
was finding it more and more difficult to comply
with the exactions of Edward the Third, and the
king himself could hardly name a day when his
very crown and jewels had not been in pawn with
the money lenders.

The less of discomfort, therefore, was felt by

3   25

Lady Maud; but she was grateful that the prince and the famous captain, Sir Walter, so frankly laughed away her apologies at their parting the next morn.

"I am but an esquire," said the prince. "My royal father biddeth me to wear plain armor and seek hard fare until I win my spurs. Thou hast given me better service than he alloweth me."

"Most noble lady," added Sir Walter, "I am proud to have been the guest of the widow of my old companion in arms——"   '

"Be thou, then, a friend to his son," she broke in earnestly.

"That will I," responded De Maunay, "but we may not serve together speedily. I go to confer with the Earl of Warwick. Then I am bidden to join Derby's forces in Guienne and Gascony. Hard goeth the war there. As for thy son, he, too, should come to Warwick with his first levies. The king hath ordered the power of the realm to gather at Portsmouth by the ninth day of next October."

"I must be there, mother," said Richard.

"Bring thy archers with thee, if thou canst," replied Sir Walter. "It is the king's thought that his next great field is to be won with the arrow, rather than the sword or the lance. But he will have only good bows, and them he will train under his own eye. It is time, now, for our going."

The young prince, like the knight, gave the respectful ceremony of departure to the Lady of Wartmont, but much of youthful frankness min-gled with his words and manner to Richard.

"I envy thee, indeed," he said to him, "thy close with the Club of Devon. I have never yet had such a fortune befall me. I have seen fights by sea and land, but ever some other hand than mine struck the best blow."

"Thou wilt strike blows enough before thou art done, thou lion's cub of England," said Sir Walter admiringly, for he loved the boy. That was good reason, too, why he was with him on this journey with so small a company.

"Few, are they?" had Richard responded to a word from his mother concerning peril to the prince. "I have marked them, man by man. I think they have been picked from the best of the king's men-at-arms. A hundred thieves would go down before them like brambles before a scythe. And the prince told me he thought it scorn to need other guards than his own people——"

"And his own sword," she said, "and the lances of De Maunay and his men. But the roads are not safe."

"Thou wilt be securely conveyed to Warwick, O my mother," he said lovingly. "I will not leave thee until thou art within the earl's own walls."

This had been spoken early in the day after

the conflict with the outlaws, and now the horsemen were in their saddles, beyond the bridge of
the moat, waiting for the prince and the knight.

Their waiting ended, and it was fair to see how
lightly the great captain and his young friend, in
spite of their heavy armor, did spring to horseback.

Gracious and low was their last salute to the
bare, white head of Lady Maud at the portal, and
then away they rode right merrily.

"O my son!" exclaimed she, turning to Richard
at her side, "I can wish no better fortune for thee
than to be the companion of thy prince. I tell
thee, thou hast won much by this thy defense of
thy mother and thy people."

"Aye," said Richard, laughing, "but thou wast
the captain. I found thee leading thy array, and I
did but help at my best. I would Sir Walter were
to be with us, and not with the Earl of Derby."

"There be men-at-arms as good as he," she said.
"Thou wilt have brave leaders to learn war under.
And, above all, thou wilt be with thy king. Men
say there hath not been one like him to lead men
since William the Norman conquered this fair land.
Thou, too, art a Neville and a Norman, but forget
thou not one thing."

"And what may that be, my mother?" asked
Richard, wondering somewhat.

"Knowest thou not thy hold upon the people,
nor why the bowmen of Arden forest come to thee

rather than to another? Neville and Beauchamp,
thou art a Saxon more than a Norman. Thy father
could talk to the men of the woods in their old
tongue. It dieth away slowly, but they keep many
things in mind from father to son. Every man of
them is a Saxon of unmixed blood, and to that degree that thou art Saxon thou art their kinsman.
So hated they Earl Mortimer and would have none
of him, and so he harried them, as thou hast heard.
They will stand by thee as their own."

"So will I bide by them!" exclaimed Richard
stoutly. "And now there is one yonder that I must
have speech with. I pray thee, go in, my mother."

"That will I not," she said. "It behooveth me
to pass through the hamlet, house by house, till I
know how they fare the day. There are hurts
among both men and women, and I am a leech.
Are they not my own?"

"And well they love thee," said her son, and
they walked on down the slope side by side.

That they did so love her was well made
manifest when men, women, and children crowded
around her. Every voice had its tale of things
done, or seen, or heard, and there was wailing
also, for the few who had escaped from near
Black Tom's place were here, and others from
farther on. Dark and dire had been the deeds
of the robber crew from the Welsh border to the
heart of Warwickshire, and great was the praise

that would everywhere be given to the young lord
of Wartmont manor and his brave men. The Club
of Devon and his outlaws would be heard of or
feared no more. 'Twas a deed to be remembered
and told of, in after time, among the fireside talks
of the midland counties.

The madame now had household visits to make
not a few, and Richard listened long to the talk of
the farmers and the village men. He seemed to
have grown older in a day, but his mother said, in
her heart:

"I can see that the folk are gladdened to find
that he is so like to the brave knight, his father.
God keep him, among the spears and the battle-
axes of the French men-at-arms! I fear he is over
young to ride with such as serve with the prince."

She could not think to hold him back, but he
was her only son, and she was a widow.

Patiently, all the while, a little apart from the
rest, had waited the burly shape of Guy the Bow,
and with him was no other forester, but beside him
stood his shaggy-maned galloway.

"Thou art come?" said Richard. "Brave thanks
to thee and thine. What errand hast thou, if so be
thou hast any for me?"

"I bided out of seeing till the prince and Lord
de Maunay rode on," replied Guy. "Even now I
would no other ears than thine were too near us."

"This way, then," said Richard, turning to walk

toward the moat. " I have somewhat to say to thee as we go."

None joined them, and as they walked the archer was informed concerning the mandates of the king and the mustering by land and sea at Portsmouth.

" I have been there," said Guy, " in my youth. 'Tis not so far to go. 'Tis well in behind the Isle of Wight. I have been told by seafaring men that the French have never taken it, though they tried. A safe haven. But there are others as safe on the land. Part of my coming to thee is to ask that thou wilt venture to look in on one."

" I may not venture foolishly or without a cause," said Richard. " Thee I may trust, but all are not as thou art."

"All thou wilt see are keepers of good faith when they give troth," laughed Guy pleasantly, " or else more in Wartmont would know what to this day they know not. My Lord of Wartmont, plain speech is best. The men who are to go with thee are under the king's ban, as thou knowest. They will not put themselves within the reach of the sheriff of Warwickshire till they are sure of safety. They will hear the king's proclamation from thine own lips, for thou hast it from the prince himself. A man's neck is a thing he is prone to guard right well."

" Go and have speech with them? That will

I!" exclaimed Richard promptly. "Nor is there time to lose. I will bid them bring my horse——"

"Not as thou now art," responded Guy. "Don thou thy mail. Be thou well armed. But men of thine from the castle may not ride with us. I have that to show thee which they may not see. Wilt thou trust me?"

"That will I," said Richard.

"And thine own sword is a good one," added the archer, with soldierly admiration in his face. "I have seen thy father in tourney. Thou wilt have good stature and strong thews, as had he in his day. They say 'twas a great battle when he fell among the press, and that many good spears went down."

"Aye. Go!" said Richard thoughtfully. "I will explain this thing to my mother. She needeth but to know that I go to meet a muster of the men."

"Nay," said Guy. "Fear thou not to tell my lady all. In her girlhood she was kept, a day and a night, where none could do her harm, for the Welsh were over the border, under Lewellyn the Cruel, and the castle of her father was not safe. She was not a Neville then, and the Beauchamps fled for their lives."

"What was the quarrel?" asked Richard.

"Little know I," replied the archer. "What have plain woodsmen to do with the feuds of

the great? Some trouble, mayhap, between King
Edward the Second and his earls. We aye heard
of fights and ravages in those days, but there came
none to harry us in Arden."

So they talked but little more, and Richard
passed on into the castle followed by Guy the
Bow.

Their first errand was to the hall of arms in the
lower story, and the eyes of the forester glittered
with delight as they entered.

"Thou couldst arm a troop!" he exclaimed.
"What goodly weapons are these!"

"Wartmont hath held a garrison more than
once," said Richard. "Pray God that our good
king may keep the land in peace. But it needeth
that his hand be strong."

"Strong is it," said Guy, "and the young prince
biddeth fair. I like him well. But, my Lord of
Wartmont, the noon draweth nigher and we have
far to ride."

"Aye," said Richard; but he was taking down
from the wall piece after piece and weapon after
weapon, eying them as if he loved them well but
was in doubt.

"No plate armor, my lord," said Guy. "It
were too heavy if thou went on foot. Let it be
good chain mail; but take thee a visored headpiece.
With thy visor down strange eyes would not know
thee too well. Leg mail, not greaves, and a good,

light target rather than a horseman's shield. This
is a rare good lance."

"That will I take," said Richard, as he tested
a sword blade by springing it on the stone pavement of the hall. "I will hang a mace at my
pommel."

"Thou art a bowman," said Guy. "Thy bow
and quiver also can hang at thy saddle. Nay, not
that heavy bit of yew. Thy arms are too young
to bend it well. Choose thee a lighter bow."

"I will string it, then, and show thee," replied
Richard, a little haughtily. "Yon is a target at the
head of the hall. Wait, now."

The bow was strung with an ease and celerity
which seemed to surprise the brawny forester. He
took it and tried its toughness and handed it back,
for Richard had taken an arrow from a sheaf beneath a window.

"Good arm, thine!" shouted Guy, for the shaft
was drawn to the head and landed in the very center
of the bull's eye of the wooden tablet at the hall
end. "Thou art a Saxon in thy elbows. Canst
thou swing an axe like this?"

He held out a double-headed battle-axe that
seemed not large. It was not too long in the
handle, but its blades were thick as well as sharp
edged. It was no weapon for one at all weak-
handed.

Clogs of wood lay near, with many cuts already

upon them, as if there had been chopping done.
Richard took the axe and went toward a clog of
hard oak.

Click, click, click, in swift succession, rang his
blows, and the chips flew merrily.

"Done!" shouted Guy. "Take that, then, instead of thy foolish mace. It will but bruise, while
thine axe will cleave through mail or buff coat.
Ofttimes a cut is better than a bruise, if it be well
given. I would I had a good axe."

"Take what thou wilt," said Richard. "Put
thee on a better headpiece, and change thy sword.
If thou seest spears to thy liking, they are thine; or
daggers, or aught else. We owe thee good arming."

"Speak I also for Ben o' Coventry," responded
Guy. "He needeth a headpiece, for his own is but
cracked across the crown, and his sword is not of
the best."

"Choose as thou wilt for Ben," said Richard,
"or for any other as good as he. Needeth he
mail?"

"His buff coat is more to his liking," said Guy,
"and men say that the king will not have his bowmen overweighted for fast walking. The weary
man draweth never a good bow, nor sendeth his
arrow home."

"Right is the king," replied Richard. "I am
but a youth, but I can see that a foe might get
away from heavy armor."

Guy was busy among the weapons and he made no answer. At that moment, however, there was a footfall behind him, and he sprang to his feet to make a low obeisance.

"Mother!" exclaimed Richard, "I was coming to tell thee."

But not to him was her speech, nor in Norman French, nor in the English dialect of the Warwickshire farmers. She questioned Guy in old Saxon, such as was not often heard since the edicts of the Norman kings had discouraged its use. Richard could speak it well, however, and he knew that Guy was explaining somewhat the errand before him.

"It is well," she said. "I will trust him with thee. The castle is safe. But hold him not too long, for I make myself ready to pass on to Warwick, to abide with the earl for a season."

"Right soon will he return," said Guy the Bow, "and good bows with him. The king shall be pleased with the company from Arden and Wartmont."

Small wonder was it, after all, that while all Welshmen retained their ancient tongue, and many Cornishmen, and the Manxmen all, and the Gaels of Scotland and the wild Erse of Ireland, so also many thousands—no one knew how many—in the rural districts of England, still preserved but little changed the language with which their fathers had answered to Harold, the last of the Saxon kings. Hundreds of years later the traces of it lingered in Warwickshire, Lincolnshire, Yorkshire, Lancashire, and elsewhere, in a manner to confuse the ears of modernized men from the towns and from the coasts, as well as all outland men who might believe that they understood English.

Well did Guy obey the commands of both Richard and his mother; for when, after a hearty breaking of his fast, he stood by the side of his galloway, that good beast had cause to whinny as he did, as if to inquire of his master what need there might be that he should so be packed with weapons and with steel caps for the heads of men. The gallant animal that was to carry Richard, on the other hand, was fitted out and laden as if at any moment his rider might be changed from a lance-bearing man-at-arms to a bowman on foot. Other baggage there was none, and Lady Maud, from her crenelated peephole in the Wartmont keep, saw her son and his companion ride slowly away through the village.

"Heaven guard him!" she murmured. "But he can not gain too well the hearts of the old race. They be hard-headed men and slow to choose a leader, but they are strong in a fray. I would the tallest of the forest deerslayers should go shoulder to shoulder with my son into the king's battles."

So she gazed until the pair of horsemen disap-

peared along the road; then she descended a
flight of stairs and walked to the end of a corridor. Here was a door that opened into a high
vaulted chamber, at the far end of which were can-
dles burning before an altar and a crucifix. This
was the chapel of the castle, and Lady Maud's feet
bore her on, more and more slowly, until she
sank upon her knees at the altar rail and sobbed
aloud.

Well away now, up the valley, northward,
rode Richard Neville and Guy the Bow, but they
were no longer in any road marked by wheels of
wains. They had left the highway for a narrow
bridle path that was leading them into the forest.

"My Lord of Wartmont," said the archer, "I
pray thee mark well the way as thou goest.
Chance might be that thou shouldst one day travel
it alone. Put thou thine axe to the bark of a tree,
now and then, and let it be a mark of thine own,
not like that of another. I think no man of
knightly race now liveth who could guide thee,
going or coming."

In an instant Richard's battle-axe was in his
hand, and a great oak had received a mark of a
double cross.

"There hangeth a shield in the gallery of the
armory," he said, "that is blazoned in this wise.
It is said that a good knight brought it home from
Spain, in the old wars. Well is it dinted, too, in

proof that it fended the blows of strong fighters. It is thrust through and it is cloven."

"Mayhap in frays with the heathen," said Guy. "A sailor, once, at Portsmouth, one of our own kin, told me rare tales of the Moors that he had seen in the Spanish seas. He told me of men that were black as a sloe; but it is hard to believe, for what should blacken any man? He had seen a whale, too, and a shark three fathoms long. There be wonders beyond seas."

"And beyond them all is the end of the world," said Richard, "but the ships do not venture that far to their ruin."

So more and more companionlike and brotherly grew the young lord and the forester, as they rode on together, and it seemed to please Guy well both to loosen his own tongue and to ask many questions concerning matters of which little telling had ever yet come in among the forests of Arden.

The day waned and the path wound much, and there was increasing gloom among the trees and thickets, when Guy turned suddenly to Richard.

"Put down thy visor," he said sharply, "and draw thy sword. We are beset! Sling thy lance behind thee, and get thee down upon thy feet. This is no place to sit upon a horse and be made a mark of."

The actions of both were suited to the word on the instant, but hardly was Richard's helmet

closed before an arrow struck him on the crest.
But that he had been forewarned, it had smitten
him through the face.

"Outlaws!" said Guy. "Robbers—not our
own men. How they came here I know not.
Down, quickly!"

Even as he spoke, however, his bow twanged
loudly, and a cry went up from a dense copse
beyond them.

"One!" he shouted, and he and Richard
sprang lightly to the earth.

"Well my sword was out!" said the latter as
he gained his feet, for bounding toward him were
half a dozen wild shapes carrying blade and buckler.

"Down with them!" roared the foremost of
the assailants; but Guy the Bow was in front of
him, and in his hand was a poleaxe from Wartmont
armory.

It was a fearful weapon in the hands of such
a man as he, to whom its weight was as a splinter.
It flashed and fell, and the lifted buckler before it
might as well have been an eggshell for all the
protection it gave to the bare head of the robber.
He should have worn a helmet, but he would never
more need cap of any kind. Useless, too, was the
light blade that glinted next upon the shield of
Richard, for it made no mark, while its giver went
down with a thigh wound, struck below his
buckler.

On swept the terrible blows of the poleaxe, and
Guy had no man to meet but was nearly a head
shorter than himself.

"They are all down!" he shouted. "Mount,
my Lord of Wartmont; they in the copse have fled,
but there may be more at hand. We will ride hard
now. These are thieves from Lancashire, and they
have not been heard of in these parts for many a
day. I think they have been harried out of their
own nests. They are but wolves."

"What kin are they?" asked Richard, as he
regained his saddle.

"That I know not, nor do I know their speech,"
replied Guy. "But among them are no tall men
nor many good bows. Ben o' Coventry hath been
told by a monk from those parts that they are a
kind of old Welsh that were left when the first
King Edward smote their tribe to death. They
will live in no town, nor will they obey any law,
nor keep troth with any. But the monk told Ben
that they were not heathen, and among them were
men who could talk Latin like a priest. How that
could be I know not."

"Nor I," said Richard; "but I tell thee, Guy
the Bow, I like this war of the king's with France.
We shall cross the sea, and we shall look upon
strange lands and towns. I would not bide aye at
Wartmont. I would see the world."

"That would not I," laughed Guy, "but if the
4

king winneth battles and taketh towns there will be spoils to bring home. I will come back to own land and cattle, and thou canst build again thy castle walls and maintain thy state. I saw a piece of gold once."

" There is little enough of gold in England," said Richard; but the path was narrowing and they could no longer gallop abreast.

Not far had they pushed on, however, before Guy drew his rein and turned upon his galloway to say, in a hushed voice:

" My Lord of Wartmont, I dare not sound a horn. I pray thee dismount and come after me through the hazels. I know not of peril, but we need to go lightly."

" Aye," returned Richard, as he dropped from the saddle nimbly enough considering his arms. " I am with thee."

Path there seemed to be none in that dim light, but ere long, as he followed his guide, the hazel bushes on either side opened widely and before him spread a grassy level. Only that the grass was too luxuriant and that here and there were rushes, it might have seemed a pleasant glade.

" 'Tis the southerly arm," said Guy, " of the great moss of Arden. There is little more of it till you get leagues north of this. Oh, but it's deep and fateful. He who steppeth into it cometh not up."

"What do we, then?" asked Richard.

"That which few may dare," replied Guy with one of his brave laughs. "But a piece onward and I will show thee. Here might be barred an army."

"That might they," said Richard, staring across the treacherous green level, below which, Guy told him, there was no bottom.

Beyond were shadowy lines that told of forest growths, and these were nearer as they led their horses onward.

"A bridge!" exclaimed Richard, as he caught a glimpse of a mass of logs and planks. "Is there crossing?"

"None but what the men of the woods can take away before dawn," said Guy. "It is a bridge that some have crossed who came not back again. I pray thee, speak not save in old Saxon. 'Tis the only tongue that may be heard inside o' the moss of Arden."

Richard spoke not aloud, but he was saying much in his thoughts.

"This, then, is the reason why the sheriff of Warwickshire had missed finding many that were traced to the forest. The takers of the king's deer know where to hide their venison. But even on this bridge a few axemen could hold back a troop. Yonder bushes could hide archery. He would be a bold captain, or crack-brained, who would lead men upon this narrow way."

The woodwork trembled somewhat with the weight of the two horses and the men, but it bore them well enough.

"Hail, thou!" came hoarsely from among the shadows as they reached the farther bank. "Come well. Thou hast him with thee."

"Greet them in Saxon," whispered Guy, and he also responded loudly:

"Hail, men, all! Is Ben o' Coventry with ye? This is Richard of Wartmont, with the king's word in his mouth. I gave him safe conduct, and his mother sendeth ye good greeting."

Something like a cheer arose from several voices, but the speakers were unseen until Guy and Richard had passed on many paces into the forest. Even then only dark and silent forms walked with them, and there were gleams of bright spearheads before them and behind.

"Every man hath his bow and his buckler," thought Richard, "and most of them are sturdy fellows. The king hath need of such. It is said that the outland men are smaller in the bones."

It was the prevailing opinion among the English of that day that one of their own was equivalent to four Frenchmen, and they counted as French nearly all of the dwellers beyond the Channel, except the Hollanders and the Danes, or

Norsemen. The Norway folk were also, by the greater part, counted as Danes, and were believed to be hard fighters. So, among the country folk, still lingered the traditions of the ancient days, when Knut and his vikings had swept the coast and conquered the island.

It was a walk of a league, and there was some talking by the way, but the men all seemed in haste and they strode rapidly.

Then they were greeted by loud shouting, and Richard saw a red light grow beyond the trees.

"Here is cleared land," was his next thought, "and yonder is a balefire. Ho! In the king's name, what is this? Are there strongholds hidden among the woods?"

Before him, as he went forward, was an open area which may have contained hundreds of acres. He could see broad reaches of it by the glaring light of a huge heap of burning wood, a few score yards from the edge of the forest. Beyond the fire, as much farther, he could discern the outlines of a large building, and, even more distinctly, a long line of palisades in front of it.

"My lord," said Guy, "yonder is the hidden ward in Arden. If any that are great of thy kins-men ever heard of it, they told thee not. There was thy mother fended, and there thy father lay long days, when Earl Mortimer's men were seeking

his head.   Thou art welcome, only let thy lips be
as our own concerning our hold.   It will be kept
well should strangers come."

Richard glanced at the rugged forms around
him, and at many more that were walking hither
and thither in the firelight.   All were armed, and
he could well believe that they would make Guy's
word good for him.   They crowded around as he
drew near, and there was an increasing heartiness
in their manner and words as he continually replied to them in the forgotten tongue.   He knew
not of gypsies, or the thought might have come to
him that these half-outlaws, every man a deerslayer,
under the ban of the stern forest laws, had need, as
had the Romany or "Bohemians" as they were
called, to possess a speech of their own.   It was a
protection, inasmuch as it aided them in detect-
ing intruders and in secretly communicating with
each other.

There seemed to be no chief man, no captain, but all stood on a kind of rude equality,
save that much deference was paid to Guy the
Bow.

"Right on to the house, if it please thee, my
lord," he said.   "It is late, and there is roast venison waiting.   Thou mayest well be hungered.   Is
all ready, Ben o' Coventry?"

"All that's to be eaten," responded Ben, "but
the talking with the men must be done on the mor-

row. They from the upper woods are not in. It was well to slay the Lancashire thieves. Some have gone out after what thou and he did leave. They may not tell tales of aught they have seen in Arden."

A few words more of explanation informed Richard that he was there sooner than had been expected, and he was quite willing to let his wild entertainers have their own way.

"I would see all," he said, "and talk to all at once."

"There might be jealousies," whispered Guy. "Thou doest wisely. Here is the gate."

A vast oaken portal heavily strengthened with iron swung open in the line of the bristling palisades while he was speaking. There was a moat, of course, with a bridge of planks to the gate, over which Richard and those who were with him went in. The inclosure beyond was large, and in it was blazing more than one log heap, the better to light up the buildings.

Some would have called it a grange, if there had not been so much of it, for there were more houses than one, all grouped, attached or built on to a central structure. There was no masonry, but the woodwork was exceedingly heavy and strong. If there were more than one story to the grange, it must have been hidden under the high-pitched roofs, for there were no upper windows. Such of these as could be seen below were all closed with heavy swing shutters, nor was there any chimney on any roof.

This was the manner in which the West Saxons of Harold's time builded the palaces of their chiefs and earls.

CHAPTER III.

WHEN Lady Maud Neville arose from her knees at the altar rail there was a beautiful light upon her noble face. Her long, white hair had fallen around her shoulders, but for some reason she seemed to have grown younger.

"I will give him to the king!" she loudly exclaimed. "I have prayed that my son may be as was his father, a knight without a stain. But here I may not tarry. It were better I made ready for a journey even ere I sleep, for when Richard returneth there will be haste. There is much that I would not leave behind. I will load no wain with goods, but the pack beasts will bear full panniers."

She walked out of the chapel and her serving men and maidens met her, eager to do her bidding. After that there were chambers and storerooms to visit and coffers to open and packs to bind, for she was not ill supplied with the garments that were suited to her rank, and above all there were small caskets of dark wood that were not opened. It

49

was said that there were gems and jewels in Wartmont, and the saying may have reached the ears of
such as Clod the Club to bring him thither. If
so, well was it that he and his would never come
again.

Ever and anon, however, as the good lady
passed a window, she would pause and look out
toward the forest, as if in that direction there
might be some one that she longed to see.

Day waned and the night came on, and all
preparations appeared to be completed, for again
she visited the chapel before retiring to her chamber. Long since had the great gate been closed,
and the portcullis lowered and the bridge over
the moat drawn in. Now, at last, the curfew bell
sounded from the tower and the lights in castle
and village went out, save one bronze lamp that
still burned in that corner of the keep to which
the lady herself had retreated.

It was a large room and lofty, with twain of
narrow windows that were as if for archers to ply
their arrows through them rather than for lighting
the space within. The floor was strewn with dry
rushes for luxury, and the garnishing was such as
became the mistress of Wartmont. Heavily carved,
of oak, were the tables and the high-backed chairs
and the settles. The mirror over the chest of draw-
ers must have come from Venice itself. There were
curtains at the windows and around the high-post

bedstead which might have been woven in Flanders or Normandy, for none such could be made in England. The walls were wainscoted to the height of a man's shoulder, but there were no tapestries to tell of great wealth. It was as if in this place of retirement had been preserved all that remained of the broken prosperity of this branch of the great house of Neville.

The lady slept not, nor even looked at the bed, but sank into a great cushioned chair and seemed to be lost in thought.

No words escaped her lips although much time went by. There was no hand to turn the hour-glass on the bureau near her, nor could she have known at what hour she was startled to her feet.

Loud rang the summoning sound of a clarion at the great gate, and louder was the sudden answer of the alarum bell in the tower. She was at a window ere she knew, and she heard a shouting:

"Open, O ye of Wartmont! In the king's name! It is John Beauchamp, Earl of Warwick. Is our lord the prince within?"

"Open will we right gladly," sent back the warder at the gate. "But the prince and my Lord of Maunay rode on to Warwick in the morn."

"Saints preserve them!" uttered another voice. "But we must needs come in. Bid the Lady Maud rest. I will trouble her not until day."

"My noble kinsman!" she exclaimed, turning

quickly from her window. "I will make haste to greet him. Well is it that I am robed. I will meet him speedily in the hall."

Even so she did, and the minutes were few before she stood face to face with a tall man of noble presence, in full armor save the helmet he had doffed on entering. He seemed in full vigor of life, but gray-headed, as became a statesman upon whom the king might lean.

Questions and answers followed fast, and all the while the Wartmont retainers were busily providing for the hundred horsemen who had ridden in the train of the earl. Of them were knights and nobles also, and some of these now stood near the lady and the earl. Strong was their speech, as was his, concerning the rashness which the prince had shown in riding across England with so small a company.

"Knoweth he not," said one, "that there is treason in the land?"

"Silence on that head, Geoffrey of Harcourt," responded the earl. "But we may trust he is safe in Warwick. Had we taken another highway we might have met him. But, madame, this is fine news of my young kinsman. Well for him that he hath won the favor of the prince and of that rare good lance, De Maunay. More than well is it also that he hath sallied forth promptly to gather his archery. It will please the king. Better bowmen are not than he will bring from Arden. Now, Lady Maud, hie thee to thy rest, and so will we all, for we are weary."

The remaining words were few, and once more the castle grew still, save for the stamping of rest-less horses in the courtyard and the busy chatter of the warders of Wartmont with the guard set by the earl.

Now there was another place in which all was quiet, only that on a heap of rushes and a spread garment lay a youth who slept not, but turned at times uneasily.

"I fear no treachery," he muttered, but not in Saxon. "I think these be true men. Yet I will leave my sword bare and my axe by it lest peril come. Who would have looked for a hold like this among these woods?"

Then his thoughts went back to that which he had seen on coming in. He had passed the moat and the portal with Guy the Bow, and through a short passage. Then he had entered a vast hall, in the middle of which blazed a fire, the smoke whereof escaped at a hole in the peak of the roof. At one end of this hall was a broad dais, two steps higher than the floor of beaten earth, and here had been spread a table for his refection. Kindly, in-deed, and full of reverence for his rank and name, had been the words and manners of all who served, for none presumed to eat with him. No other man was there of gentle blood, and even Guy the Bow would have been angered had any trespassed upon his young captain. That was Richard, now, by the command of the prince himself, and the forest-men all honored the king, Saxons though they were. None were permitted to question, overmuch, although Guy himself went out to dispense what-ever news was in his own keeping.

Refreshed, even with a tankard of ale that was brought him, Richard arose at last, and followed Ben of Coventry to the sleeping place allotted him. None better was in the grange. If at any past day there had been more costly furniture, some hand had taken it away, and naught was left now but safe quarters for such men as Richard had seen.

It was but day dawning when a hunter's horn sounded a clear note at the door of the rude chamber.

"Hail, my Lord of Wartmont!" spoke Guy the Bow. "I pray thee hasten. Thy men will be ready for thee within the hour. They all have come, and they are eager to hear thee."

"On the moment!" shouted Richard. "I am ready. Tell them I come."

"God speed thee this day," said Guy. "Full many a good fellow is ready to free himself from peril of the sheriff of Warwickshire. Aye, and to draw the king's good pay and have chance for pil-laging French towns. They like it well."

Great indeed was the astonishment of Richard when, after hurriedly breaking his fast in the great hall, he walked out with Guy and others like him to view the gathering in the open space beyond the palisades.

Women and children, score on score, kept at a little distance, but not beyond hearing. In the middle, however, were clustered fully a hundred brawny men, eager to hear the king's proclamation of free pardon and enlistment for the war in France. They all knew what it was to be from other tongues, but to them the young lord of Wartmont was the king's messenger, and there was no certainty in their minds until he had spoken.

Without too many words, but plainly and well, did he announce his message, and they answered him with loud shouting. To some of them it was as a promise of life from certain death, for the law was in search of them, and the judges of that day were pitiless concerning forestry and the protection of the king's deer and the earl's.

Short ceremony was needed, for man after man came forward to kneel and put his hands between those of Richard, in the old Saxon custom of swearing to be his men in camp and field, in fight and foray, in the inland and the outland, until the king's will should give them grace to come home again.

Born warriors were they all, and they laughed

with glee in the hope of fighting the French under
so good a leader as was Edward of England. Good
captain, good success, they knew ; and as for Richard, had they not known the knight, his father,
and had not he himself slain the Club of Devon in
single-handed combat ? They were proud to serve
under a Neville, and a man of their Saxon blood,
who could order them in their own tongue.

"One hundred and one !" shouted Guy at last.
"May I not bid them to horse, Lord Richard ?
Every man can have his own galloway, or another,
that the road to the camp at Warwick may be
shortened."

"Mount !" shouted Richard. His own gallant
steed had been led to his side and in a moment
more he was in the saddle.

John, Earl of Warwick, was also early upon his
feet, for he was a man whose life had been spent
much in camps, and he was wont to be out and
using his eyes as a captain before breaking his fast.
From the men of Wartmont he speedily learned all
relating to the raid of the Club of Devon and the
brave fight made in front of the castle. Of this
also he noted the defects, and he roundly declared
that he would soon give command and provide
means for its repair.

"We may need it again some day," he said to
himself. "There may be stormy times to come.
May God prevent strife at home, but there be over-

proud hearts and over-cunning heads in this good
land of ours. I will see to it that Wartmont shall
be made stronger than ever. Glad am I that Sir
Edward Neville hath left so brave a son to stand
for our house."

Many and bitter were the jealousies of the high-
hearted barons of England, and none could tell the
days to come. Who should prophesy how long
the reigning house might keep the throne, or between what claimants of the crown might be the
next struggle, if, for example, King Edward or his
son, or both of them, and their next of kin, should
go down in battle or should die suddenly in their
beds, as others of royal blood had died? The
head of a great baronial house might well bethink
himself of every advantage or possible peril.

"But for the poverty the war bringeth," he
said, "I would have builders here within the week.
As it is, I will have a garrison, and the good dame
herself must bide at Warwick while her son is
with the army in France. 'Twere shame to leave
her here alone."

So said he to Lady Maud when they met in
the castle, and she told him then how well prepared she was for a departure. Already was she
aware of his reason for coming so far to meet the
prince; but his anxiety was at an end, and he was
willing to linger and make full his soldierly inspection of the castle.

5

"Good fort," he said, "and well was it held against Earl Mortimer. Glad am I that thy son hath so good control of the forest men. They are as clannish as are the Scotch, and they will come to their own chief when they will bide no other."

He understood them, but he was yet taken by surprise before the noon.

"Horsemen!" he exclaimed, standing in the gateway. "Rightly did I say there was imprudence in the small company of the prince. Yonder is a troop—yea, twain of them."

No lances were visible, but at the head of the foremost troop rode one who carried on a high staff a blue banneret, and the earl knew not as yet what its blazonry might be.

Truth to tell, it was nothing but an old flag of Sir Edward Neville's which had been stowed away in the crypts of the grange. Not all of these had been inspected by Richard, but he had seen a good smithy wherein galloways were shod, and spear-heads and arrowheads and knife blades were hammered and tempered. Not only arrowsmiths were there among the forest men, but good bowyers, that they might not depend for their weapons upon any but themselves. Weaving, too, was done among the women and by skilled websters of the men; but shoemakers or cordwainers they had none, and but rough potters and smelters. So dwelt they as best they might, with cattle and sheep and swine, and the black cattle of the woods and the king's deer for their maintenance. They were not at any time in peril of starvation, for excellent also were the fishes in the pools and streams, and there was no end of skilled brewing of ale.

Four and four abreast rode on the mounted archers who had sworn to come to the king with Richard of Wartmont, and they came on right orderly. Well looked he also, in full armor, at their head.

" 'Tis Richard, my lord the earl!" called out to him Lady Maud as they rode nearer. " 'Tis my brave son and his men! Believest thou now that he can call the men of the woods? My boy! God bless him!"

" That say I!" loudly responded the earl, striding across the moat-bridge. " Ho, all! Get ready for the way. My lady, I pray thee to go in and lade thy pack beasts. We will even march for Warwick ere the day is an hour older."

Loud and hearty was his cousinly greeting to his young kinsman. Strong was his approval of the force he had enlisted, but he added:

" What shall we do with all these beasts? The king will have his archers on their own feet."

" That is provided for," replied Richard. " I pray thee trust me that the whole drove can go back to Arden, under good driving, as soon as there is no more need for them. I deemed it

well to come quickly. Such was the word given
me by Sir Walter de Maunay."

"Thou didst well to heed him," said the earl;
but then he talked little more with Richard.

He bade the men dismount and get their noon-
day meal in the village and in the castle; but he
had speech with many of them, for he was well
pleased that such a company should come to the
royal standard from among his own retaining.

Lady Maud had waited, but not all patiently,
for her own greeting to her son. It was a joy to
both of them that they were to go on to Warwick
together, but most of all that a better day seemed
to be dawning for them, and that the ruin wrought
by the bad Earl Mortimer might be amended.

Not many men had been left behind in the
hidden hold amid the forest, and such as had not
marched with Richard had long since dispersed.
Some had ridden gayly away on their stout ponies;
others had gone to the fields. Some were in the
smithy, the tannery, and the other workshops, and
a few had restlessly snatched bows and arrows to
hurry out into the woods as hunters.

No guards were set, except that a pair of bowmen lingered on the farther side of the causeway
over the morass. There was little peril of intru-
sion now that the Lancashire Welsh thieves had
been sorely smitten. Whatever might remain of
them would not return to be shot down.

As for the secret character of the grange itself, there was small wonder that a few hundred acres, if so much there might be, of patches of farm land should be sheltered among those woods from any but such men as had been Sir Edward Neville. It might all be within the somewhat doubtful borders of his own manorial grant, given to his ancestors by the earlier kings and confirmed by Edward the First, to be lost under his son, the second Edward, and Earl Mortimer, and to be regained under Edward the Third and the house of Beauchamp.

It was said, indeed, that there were regions tenfold as wide, in some of the remoter baronies, whereof men knew but little, especially among the Scottish border counties and among the hills. Besides these were the unsearched fen districts on the coasts, the wild mountain parts of Wales, and worst of all were the highlands of Scotland and the sea-girt isles of the Scottish coasts. As for Ireland, even the greater part of it was almost an unknown land to Englishmen, for nothing less than an army might venture inland too far with any hope of ever coming back again.

In the several parts of the grange itself, as in the cottages scattered beyond it, the women plied their tasks. Some of them spun with distaffs, and two or three looms were busy; more might have been but for the lack of wool. There was much raising of sheep in the more thickly settled parts

of England in those days, but there was small room
for them in Arden. Moreover, they, more than
cattle or horses or swine, were sorely thinned by
the wolves. It was a hundred and fifty years later
that these fierce beasts disappeared from England,
and the last of them in Scotland was slain yet a
century later. So was it that so little cloth, even
of homespun, was worn by the bowmen who rode
behind Richard of Wartmont, in the gloom of that
evening when he followed the Earl and his men-
at-arms through the gate of Warwick town.

Long had been the journey, hard pushed and
weary were beasts and men. There was small
ceremony of arrival or reception for the greater
part of the cavalcade, but the Lady Maud was
conducted at once to the care of the Countess
Eleanor of Warwick, her younger sister, the wife
of the earl.

As for Richard, his men were cared for well,
under direction of Sir Geoffrey de Harcourt,
while their young captain was bidden to hasten
with his great kinsman to meet once more the
Prince of Wales and Sir Walter de Maunay.

This greeting, too, was brief, for the hour was
late ; but the prince said graciously :

"O thou of Wartmont, I will make thee my
comrade in arms! In the morn I would fain see
thy men. My father himself bade me gather as
many deer stealers as I might, for, quoth he, the

hand that can send a gray goose shaft to strike a stag at a hundred yards may fairly bring down a Frenchman at half that distance. Give me bow-men enough of the right sort, and I will train them to face anything that Philip of France can muster."

"O my Lord the Prince," replied Richard, "I have a hundred with me, of whom any man can send an arrow through a coat of mail at fifty yards. I like the king's notion right well."

"Go, now," said the prince; "go with thy kinsman, the earl. On the morrow I will tell thee what to do with *thy* men."

But these, for their part, were all of a merry heart that night. Not often had any of them visit-ed Warwick, at least in later years, for therein was a jail, and they liked not so much as to look thereon, being in danger of being put within it. They had good quarters and good fare, with much ale, and they knew they were to see brave sights next day, and to have a word from even the Black Prince himself. Was not that enough of cheer for men of the woods who had seldom been out beyond the shadows of the oaks of Arden?

The stout earl and his nephew walked together from the presence of the prince toward the chamber allotted to Richard.

"Thou shalt be to me as a son!" exclaimed the earl, in the dim corridor through which they were

pacing. "Thou hast won the prince. Now, if thou
wilt go and win thy spurs with him, thy fortune is
made. Thou wilt have broader lands than Wartmont, but wert thou even to win much gold, I bid
thee bide by thine own keep and hold to thee thy
Saxon men. If thou wilt do so, I can foresee the
day when thou canst bring five hundred bowmen
to the standard of thy house."

"I can bring but four more men-at-arms now,"
said Richard ruefully.

"And thy archers?" laughed the earl. "Didst
thou not hear Geoffrey Harcourt say to Northampton, that if all the great barons of England would
do as well as thou hast done, the array of the king
would be gathered right speedily? Too many are
afraid to leave their own domains lightly guarded,
and, truth to tell, not a few are carrying slender
purses. The drainings of these long wars have
made us poor. I am myself in the hands of the
Jews and the London Lombards for more debts
than I can see how to pay. So is the king, and
he is troubled in mind as to how he shall feed and
pay his armies. Go to thy couch and arise right
early. Beware that thou never keep the prince
waiting. He is like his royal father, and he who
would fail of meeting the king hath gone near to
making him a sworn enemy. His temper is dan-
gerous. See that thou arouse him not at any time.
His hand is hard upon men, and so will any troops

of his be disciplined as were never English troops since William won the island."

If that were to prove true, it might be one of the reasons why the king so firmly believed that he could bring the men so disciplined face to face with greater numbers of the disorderly levies of his rival, the King of France.

The stern counsel of the wise earl was hardly needed, so far as Richard's early rising was concerned, but he was up not any too soon in the morn. Nor was he any too mindful of his duty as a soldier of the king. He arose and put on his armor and walked out of his chamber, and before him stood an archer.

"The commands of the earl," he said bluntly. "Eat not, but hasten to thy men. They break their fast even now. Have thou them in line right speedily. I will be thy guide to their quarters."

"I obey the earl," said Richard, following.

It was not far to go, beyond the castle gate, and Richard turned for a moment to gaze back upon towers and battlemented walls which had resisted so many a stout assailing.

"They are held for the king now," he thought, "but they once were held against him, and oft against other kings. In yonder dungeon keep hath more than one proud earl been brought to the block, and men say that in it, even now, are prisoners of note that may never again see the day."

Dark and high and threatening was the aspect of the great keep of Warwick Castle, and there might be terrible secrets of state in its under-ground chambers.

He turned again to follow the archer, but when he came to the quarters of his troop, he found that the commands of the earl were there before him. The forest men were used to be up with the dawn, and it had been no surprise to them to find their tables ready spread. Also, they liked the fare, and they were in good heart when they came out to greet their young captain. They cheered him loudly; but a new thought flashed into his mind.

"Soldiers? Drilled?" he said to himself. "I see what the earl means. They all can shoot well, but they can neither form line nor move together, nor do they know the words of command. The prince—is he here thus early?"

Here he came, the heir of the crown of Eng-land and of the English claim to the crown of France. He was in his plain black armor, with his visor raised, but on his face was no smile of youthful familiarity—rather, something of the hard look that distinguished his father and that made men fear him; and the hardness was in his voice as well, when he shouted swift orders to Richard.

Low had been his obeisance, but he had a bitter feeling in his heart, for he knew not how to form his men. All he could do was to turn to them and shout:

"Follow!"

"By fours! Spears in line!" added Guy the Bow, and more words in Saxon bade them hold their shields in front and step together.

Less shame felt Richard when he saw how well they came on, and the lips of the prince relaxed somewhat.

"Not a rabble," he muttered. "They will train well. I never saw new men move thus. The Neville doeth better than I thought. I will speak to the earl."

Other knights were with him, gallantly mounted all, and behind him they rode out to the broad common of Warwick, for there was to be a morning review of the earl's retainers and of levies which had arrived.

Never before had Richard seen together three thousand armed men, horse and foot, and greatly delighted by so rare a show were his woodsmen. In large part these forces had already been well trained by the officers of Earl Warwick, and the prince himself ordered them through many movements, such as might be needed upon a field of battle.

A rare man was Guy the Bow, for he and Ben of Coventry had been trained in their time, and they had instructed their comrades at the grange in days gone by, and the rest on the way as they came. So was it that when Richard of Wartmont led his two fifties hither and thither, he and they were a further surprise to the prince and to his captains and noble knights. They fell not into any confusion at any point, and again it was said of them, "No rabble," and "The Wartmont doeth well for a beginner."

After that, archery butts were set up and squads from several companies were picked, by lot only, and ordered to show their skill.

Right good was the shooting, as might have been expected, for there were prizes as well as praises to be won; but at the noon, when all was over, it was found that every best shot, save one, on all the butts had been made by the slayers of the king's deer in Arden.

"O thou of Wartmont," laughed Sir Walter de Maunay, "I think thou wert wise in asking so many pardons! Thy merry men are in good practice."

So laughed the prince, but there had been counseling that day and he now summoned Richard to himself. With him were the Earl of Warwick and four other earls, and Richard felt sorely abashed before he was spoken to.

"What sayest thou, John Beauchamp of War-wick?" he heard the prince demand. "What wouldst thou with the levies?"

"My Lord the Prince," responded the earl, "even as seems to me to have been said by the king. We must hear from Scotland. The king crosseth not the channel before winter. Neither will he keep too many thousands, at great cost and loss, in the Portsmouth camp."

"What then?" asked the prince.

"As for my nephew's men," said the earl, "they are too few—gathered in a day. Instead of one hundred, he will bring twain or more. Keep these for a week, and send them to recruit their fellows. Thou knowest the power of the Neville name among them. Send Richard to York."

"Good counsel!" exclaimed the prince. "Richard of Wartmont, select thee a dozen of thy trustiest men on thy best galloways. Be thou with them two hours hence, at the castle gate. Thou shalt be the king's post bearer to his Grace the Archbishop of York, and to the barons of the north counties."

Richard bowed low, flushing with pride and joy, for the spirit of travel and of adventure swelled high within him.

"Thanks to thee, O my Prince!" was all that he could say, and he went back among his men.

CHAPTER IV.

THE prince was but a youth, although of good stature and strongly made. From his cradle up he had been trained under the care of the stout king, his father, and of knights who were chosen from the best swords and bravest hearts in England. Assured was he that only a hardy soldier and a good general might safely keep the crown. The barons of the realm—half kings in their own domains—had proved the ruin of the second Edward, and only by deep cunning and ruthless force had the third of the name broken loose from a like thraldom. Much blood had been shed before the scepter was firmly in his grasp ; and a fiercely royal self-will had been instilled into the Prince of Wales as one of the safeguards of his kingship. Therefore, when sent to Warwick to confer concerning the mustering of the forces, he had come there to command as well as to take counsel.

"My Lord of Harcourt," he said with much dignity to that noble warrior, "I have listened

well to all that hath been said. Plain is it that the
earl is right. There will be no crossing to France
with King David of Scotland threatening the border counties. We must hear from the Archbishop
of York. I will send the Wartmont. He will go
and come right speedily."

There was he now in front of the castle gate,
with Guy the Bow and ten more of the archers
of Arden. To Richard himself had been given a
fresh horse and good, with two pack beasts well
laden, for the king's especial post might make a
good show at any castle or town he should come to
on his way. So was it with his merry men all, for
their buff coats were new and they covered each a
doublet of green cloth. All their galloways were
saddled and bridled, with fair housings, and one of
them carried a lance and a pennon, whereon were
blazoned a white star and cross, and over them a
gilded crown, in token of their errand. Woe to
any who should dare to hinder a messenger of the
king, or fail to speed him on the king's errand!

Not that Richard himself knew the meaning of
the letters that were in his pouch, nor that matters
of state were in his head. But a proud band and
merry were the bowmen who rode behind him out
of the town gate and up the highway to the northward.

"O my Lord of Wartmont!" said Guy the
Bow. "This is better than I had hoped. I had

not so much cared to see the outland folk, but I had hungered for a look at more of England."

"Thou art out of the woods now," replied Richard, "and so am I, but there is little more for us than riding from sleep to sleep, and caring well for our beasts. We may not pause under any roof longer than to break our fast and let the galloways rest."

"We can see as we go," said Ben of Coventry. "A man learneth much by what he seeth. But half the archers of Arden would come at the king's call, if they knew how well they would be taken in hand."

That truly was the wisdom of the prudent Earl of Warwick, and it suited the humor of the prince, for from all the land the levies had been slow in gathering. As for himself, his stay in Warwick was to be of the briefest, for he had learned many things to carry to the ears of his royal sire at London.

Well went it with the Lady Maud after she had spoken a short farewell to her son that day, for she was now housed with kindred and with many noble ladies, and was hearing tidings of the world that could not have reached her at Wart-mont. Moreover, there were new fashions of dress and equipage that all women love to learn, and the stately dame herself had brought with her goodly fabrics ready for shaping by the skilled needle-

women of her sister, the countess. It was better
than being cooped almost alone in the gloomy old
keep at Wartmont.

A day and a night, and a day and then another
night, lingered the prince. His main business
seemed to be with the levies, and he said to himself :

"I will know them man by man, and so will
the king, my father. I will measure with care the
force wherewith we are to meet Philip of France.
The king is most of all wary concerning his bowmen. I like well the Wartmont's tall deer stealers.
They are worth a pardon. We must have more of
them. I, too, must be seen in Wales. Would that
I could drain out of it the most unruly spirits and
the fiercest outlaws. So is the king's command
concerning Ireland. If any rogue there is worse
than another, let him be brought in and put in
training."

Deep was the craft of the king, therefore, and
of the prince, for if any wild man came at their
call, and they liked not the promise of his thews
and sinews, him they took not, after testing him,
for he might be no better than one of the peasants
of the King of France, fitter to dig than to carry
sword and buckler.

The summer days went by, even as Richard
had told his men. Steadily, even hastily, they
pressed their northward way, and tower and town

6

gave them hearty welcome. There were those who
unduly asked what their errand might be, but to
noble or simple there was but one reply:

"Ask thou the king, if thou wilt meddle with
his business."

There were earls and barons, of course, to
whom was due great courtesy of speech, and, indeed, to all ears there was much free news to tell.
Ever, as they went farther on, they heard more
rumors of the doubtful state of things upon the
Scottish border.

"There was never peace there," said the Earl
of Arundel, at the gate of a castle where Richard
met with him and other noble lords. "King
David will be in England within a week from the
sailing of the English fleet. Young sir, tell thou
this from me to the good archbishop. Bid him send
few levies to the king from the north counties, but
hold a force in waiting that shall be as good as any
the king may convey to France. Else we shall see
the thistles of Scotland halfway to London town
before he can meet the lilies of France in any field
beyond the sea."

Richard bowed low, for he was abashed before
so grand a company; but he had not ridden far before he heard Ben of Coventry assuring Guy the
Bow, with his usual freedom:

"Right wise was yonder earl, thou fat-head.
But doth he deem that the king hath forgotten

Scotland? Trust thou him for that. Ah me, that we must go and come and never kill a Scot!"

"Or be killed by them," said Guy. "Keep thy head for the French to hack at. Thou wilt get knocks enough."

"Mayhap," said Ben; "but I say one thing: Never did twelve men from Arden fare so well for no harder work than riding. It payeth me to serve the king. We have been feasted all the way."

"Wert thou in Scotland," laughed Guy, "it were otherwise. They eat but oatmeal cakes, and they know not of ale. I wonder much if they have deer in such a land where all is fog and mist, and where the days are short at both ends. But the Scotch fight hard, and sorely would they harry England were a chance given them."

They seemed to be at peace at that time, but King Edward and his advisers had rightly read the state of affairs in the kingdom over which David the Bruce was but half a king. No check had as yet been given to the power of the great Scottish baronial houses. They were beyond the control of any man, and David had inherited his father's valor without either the generalship or the prudence of the great Robert the Bruce.

It was at last in the morning of a fair, warm day that Richard and his archers rode out from under a dense wood to shout together as one man for what they saw.

"Aye, here we are!" said Richard, "and yonder is the spire of York Cathedral. One hour more and we are at our journey's end."

Never before had any man among them journeyed so far, but they showed small signs of wear or weariness. Nevertheless, at Richard's command they gave goodly attention to their apparel and their weapons, and to the coats of their beasts, before presenting themselves at the gate of the ancient cathedral city.

"I have heard tell," said Richard to Guy, "that here was a town in the old days of the Romans. There hath been many a battle and leaguer before these walls."

"The Romans?" replied Guy. "I was told of them by a Cornish man. There were giants in Cornwall in those days. God grant they are all gone their way; but the Cornish men say they at times find the long bones and the big, hollow skulls."

"The gates are well guarded," was the next thought of Richard. "Can there be bad news from the north?"

Guards there were, and none went out or in without notice to discern well whom they might be, as if, perchance, there were spies in the land.

"In the king's name!" shouted Richard, at the

gate, "Richard of Wartmont. From Earl Warwick and the king's duty to his Grace the Archbishop."

"In the king's name, enter!" as loudly responded a crested knight who had advanced before the
sentries. "Follow thou me to the archbishop. The
warders will care for thy men. I am Robert Johnstone of the Hill. Art thou not a Neville, and my
kinsman?"

"That am I," said Richard. "My father was
Sir Edward Neville."

"Good knight and true," responded Sir Robert.
"I have fought at his side. There must needs be
a rare message when thy uncle the earl chose thee
for his postboy."

"Words must be few," said Richard, "but now
I know who thou art, I will tell——"

"Tell not!" interrupted the knight. "Do I
not discern thy pennon? Name not any who were
with the earl until thou hast emptied thy postbag.
Thou art but young, and these be treacherous times.
A brave band are thy men——"

"Archers of my own company," said Richard,
a little proudly. "Every man from the forests of
Arden."

"And every man a born retainer of Sir Edward
Neville's house," laughed Johnstone. "Do I not
know thee and thine? We will have speech together soon, where there may be no other ears.

The Johnstones are as thou art, the chiefs of old clans that the new men can do naught with."

Great then was the surprise of the young messenger when his sudden acquaintance talked to him in Saxon, bidding him also not to use that speech except among his own, and telling him that the north counties contained more than did the midlands of such men as had preserved jealously the memories of the days of Harold the Saxon.

" 'Tis a tough race," said the knight. " It is a good foundation for thy house to rest upon. Aye, or for the king's throne. Now, if thou wilt dismount, yonder esquire will care for thy horse."

Sir Robert appeared to be acting as captain of warders, and none questioned or hindered him as he and Richard walked on, side by side, toward the castlelike palace which served as the residence of the archbishop. The town was the largest, and its buildings were the best that Richard yet had seen. He knew, moreover, that the learned prince of the Church before whom he was about to stand was also accounted second to none among the statesmen of England, with rare capacity for affairs of war as well as of peace. He was a man, therefore, to whom might be intrusted the safety of a realm in the absence of its king, and in him had Edward the Third unshaken confidence as being loyal and true.

Word of their coming had gone on before them

swift-footed, and they were ushered with all haste
into the great hall where his Grace was already
present, for the reception of they knew not what
or whom.

At the upper end of the hall, upon a raised dais
of three steps, was a throne chair, carved richly with
emblems of the Church, and surmounted by a high
cross that seemed of silver. In front of this, clad
gorgeously in flowing robes, stood the archbishop,
and before him knelt a knight in splendid armor,
but bareheaded, just on the point of rising. The
quick eyes of the prelate flashed keenly, and he
turned to an attendant monk.

"Anselmus," he said in Latin, "bring hither
yonder messenger. I must read his letters before
I have further speech with Douglas."

"He hath summoned thee," whispered Sir
Robert to Richard. "Speak not at all to him,
lest thou err greatly. Yon is the knight of Liddesdale, the prowest spear of Scotland. His presence
bodeth no good to England, I fear."

The monk came and touched Richard's arm and
led him forward. Glad was he of his injunction
not to speak, for he was greatly awed to be in that
presence. He walked onward with bowed head,
and on the dais he knelt before the archbishop.

"Thy letters, my son," said the prelate.

Not a word spoke Richard, but he silently presented three sealed missives. One he knew was

from the prince, one from the Earl of Warwick, and the third was to him a secret. Nevertheless he heard the archbishop mutter:

"The king's own hand?"

Then he said aloud:

"Wait thou here, my son. Rise; I will return presently. My Lord Douglas, come thou with me into my cabinet."

Richard arose and stood in his place, but it seemed not long before the archbishop strode back again, and with him came the knight of Liddesdale.

"Your Grace," said the latter, "I ride within the hour."

"Peace go with thee," responded the archbishop. "Peace be with thee and thine; with thy king and my king; with Scotland and with England! Amen!"

Then from all who were present came a responsive Amen, as the knight knelt for a parting blessing and rose to depart.

"Come thou, my son Richard," said the archbishop. "I would hear thee."

It was strange fortune for a youth so inexperienced to find himself mingling in affairs so tremendous, and Richard hardly breathed until he was alone with the great man in a kind of oratory wherein was an altar.

"Speak!" said the archbishop. "Tell all."

First, then, Richard told of the prince and
De Maunay at Wartmont, and the archbishop
answered not save to mutter:

"So! thou hast slain that wolf, the Club of
Devon. Thou art like thy father."

Then told Richard not of the grange in the
woods, but of his going to Warwick with his archers, and again he heard the prelate mutter, but in
Saxon:

"Saxons, all! How we of the old blood do
cling together! He doeth well."

All the words of the prince and of those with
him were repeated, but no comment was made.
After that told Richard the saying of the Earl of
Arundel, and he had finished.

"Well for thee, my son," said the archbishop.
"Thou hast seen Lord Douglas. He is for peace.
Mark me, I will write letters. Thou wilt bear
them. Wait in York till they are given thee.
Come not to me unless I summon thee. I note
that thou rememberest clearly, and canst carry that
which may not be written. This, then, say to the
king or to the prince, but not to another save John
Beauchamp the earl, lest thou die. Bid the king
from me that Douglas and his friends will fail in
their counsels for peace. David of Scotland is for
war, and waiteth but opportunity. He must now
have one. Edward the King will not but seem to
drain of force these northern counties, that the Scot-

tish lords may deem them unguarded. He will gather an army for his war in France. Such another will we prepare to meet the Scottish invasion. Let the king be sure that when he saileth for France the Scottish host will march for the English border. Edward will prove too much for so rash a man, with all his cunning, as is Philip of France. In like manner we will prove too much for David of Scotland, who despiseth the warnings of men like Douglas of Liddesdale. We will crush the Scottish invasion, taking the unwise in a snare. Go!"

Deep was the reverence with which Richard turned to depart. More words were given him, however, and much was his wonder at a man who seemed to know the thoughts of the hearts of other men, and to read the forces of the kingdoms as if he were counting pennies.

A good monk led the young messenger out of the hall and gave him into the care of Sir Robert Johnstone.

"Say not too much to me," said the knight. "I talked with Liddesdale, and heavy of heart is he. A wise man as well as a good captain; but the Scots must learn a lesson. How long tarriest thou in York?"

"For letters only," said Richard.

"Then bide with me, and let thy men rest and their beasts. I will show thee the town and the castle and the cathedral. 'Tis a grand old town. I like it well."

"I shall like well to see," said Richard. "But how great is the archbishop! Never before have I looked into the face of such a man."

"Wait, then, until thou hast seen the king," replied Sir Robert. "Try if thou canst read him. Thou wilt be with the prince."

Out they went, and Richard's eyes were so busy that he found small use for his tongue. Nor was there great need, save for a question here and there, for the knight had taken a liking to him and was willing to instruct him.

"Some day," he said, "thou mayest lead thy archery hitherward. Spare not to learn aught that might serve thee if thou wert a captain, in whatever land thou shalt at any time visit."

At the close of the day, when the vespers were ringing sweetly in the cathedral tower, Richard was with his men, and they gathered around him gladly, telling how well they had fared.

"Guy the Bow," laughed Richard, "tell me truly, now, of those who have been with thee. Hast thou broken thy jaws with French or north English, or hast thou chattered in Saxon?"

The laugh was echoed from man to man, and Guy the Bow responded :

"Now, my lord, knowest thou this already? There be more of the old sort here than in Warwickshire. They tell that there be many Nevilles hereaway, and it seemed right to them that one of thy house should be our captain. But I hear that the bowmen of these parts are to be kept at home."

"Say not too much of that to any man," said Richard, for at once he remembered the words of the archbishop.

"The king," he thought, "will deal with the Scots as with the French. They must get their teaching from the longbow and the cloth-yard arrow."

Rest came well that night after so long a journey. The next day, and the next, were but spent in seeing sights and in waiting for orders. On the third day, however, before the sun was a half hour high, came Sir Robert Johnstone to greet his young friend.

"Up, Richard of Wartmont!" he gayly shouted. "Take thou this pouch and keep it with thy life until thou shalt deliver it to the king's hand. Thine uncle the earl, or the prince, shall be to thee as the king, but on thy life and on thy head give it to no other."

The parcel was small and it was tightly bound in dressed deerskin. It could be hidden under a coat of mail, and there did Richard at once conceal it.

"I will but break my fast," he said. "Then we will mount and ride."

"Beware of overhaste," said the knight. "Safety is more than speed in such a case as this. A day more or less will not matter. Thou wilt know enough not to talk loosely by the way, but it is from his Grace himself that thou shalt speak only of peace with Scotland. Baron or earl or common, all must rest assured that the Scots are weary of war. Well they might be, were there wisdom in them. I would their king were older. We shall beat them the more easily because he putteth aside such captains as the Knight of Liddesdale, and listeneth to hot-headed young chiefs that never yet saw a thousand spears in line."

"Thou wilt be here?" said Richard.

"That will I," replied the Johnstone. "The king will hear a good report of his north country bowmen. If thou speakest of it to the prince, say this from me, that in his own camp there shall be no better discipline nor closer archery."

Rapid was their talking, but when they summoned Richard's men there was a shout. They had seen enough of York already, and they were eager for the road. To them all it was more like a long junketing than aught else.

"All Arden would list," said Ben of Coventry, "for this sort of war service. But I had hoped somewhat for a brush with the Scots. Not an arrow hath sped since we set forth from Warwick."

"Thou wilt have archery enough before thou art done with the king's war," replied Richard.

"Mind thou thy galloway, Ben," interrupted Guy the Bow. "What knowest thou of the Scots? They are many a league away."

"Aye, man," said Ben, "and all the Yorkshire men know that Douglas of Liddesdale was here. All Scotland may march behind him some day."

"Then I may say to thee," said Richard, "and to every man of this company, speak not upon the way one word of the Knight of Liddesdale. Closed lips, safe head. We are on the king's errand."

"Even so!" exclaimed Ben. "I was right. I deemed the Scottish captain a bird of ill omen. Thou mayest trust thy men, Lord Richard of Wartmont. We of the greenwood are well used to keeping a silent tongue. Else were our necks worth but little."

Richard said no more; but it was well that he had with him none but trusty companions, for all their journey homeward would be beset by shrewd questioners eager to get the latest tidings from the north.

"I will take another road," he thought, "than that by which I came. There are roads plenty. The Earl of Arundel will be at Warwick when I get there, or at London."

Hearty was the farewell of Sir Robert John-

stone at the city gate, and gay was the setting
forth of Richard and his men. But it was even
according to the saying of wise Ben of Coventry,
that an esquire and eleven archers were riding a
holiday with nothing to do but to ride and to be
hailed at every gateside to tell what news.

Even the second day passed in like manner,
and it was far on in the third when the first hap-
pening came.

Not in any town or by any castle, but in the
broad highway, there rode to meet them a glittering array of men-at-arms.

"Halt!" shouted Richard. "Form line at the
roadside, till we know what this may mean. Yonder is a banner with the arms of Surrey. Why
should such a flag be here? I know not the earl,
nor is he a friend of the Warwick, Beauchamp or
Neville."

So many, in those troubled days, were the
feuds and heartburnings among the stout barons
of England!

On came the lances, fully a score, with mounted
esquires and serving men as many, and Richard sat
alone upon his horse in the roadway, with Guy the
Bow at his side bearing the prince's pennon.

Sharply the men-at-arms drew rein, and only
one knight spurred forward.

"Richard of Wartmont!" he exclaimed. "Glad
am I thou camest this way. They who wait thee

on the other road must not know thy errand. Surrey is not here, but the Earl of Northampton."

"My Lord of Harcourt," responded Richard
firmly, "I may not answer even thee, nor give my
errand save to our liege the king, or to the prince."

"Thou wouldst deserve to lose thy head if thou
didst," replied Sir Geoffrey of Harcourt. "Do
thou, however, as if the prince bade thee. Go not
to Warwick, but send thy archery there. Turn
thou with me and ride for thy life until thou art
out of reach of the king's enemies."

"Guy the Bow," said Richard, turning to him,
"hast thou heard?"

"If it be also thy command," said Guy, "fear
not for us. Little do we need of highways or of
any man's permission. Let me have speech with
the men."

"Bid them to reach Warwick town as best
they may," said Richard.

To the roadside and to his company went Guy,
and in a few moments more he raised a hand, and
the few words he spoke were in Saxon.

Up again went the hand of Richard, with a
loud "Ha! Ride!"

Now at that place was a great forest, with a
deep ditch along the roadside.

As Richard lowered his hand, over the ditch
went the line of galloways, and it was but a twink-
ling before all had vanished among the trees.

"Wartmont," exclaimed the knight, "thou hast thy men well in hand! I will tell the prince of this. Thou canst call them and thou canst send them."

"How is this?" loudly demanded a not un-kindly voice, as another rider in splendid armor rode near them.

"My Lord of Northampton," said Sir Geoffrey, smiling, "Richard hath sent home his galloways, and they took their riders with them. He must not pause——"

"A few words only," said the earl; "I shall not hinder the king's service. Arundel gave thee a message. Was it delivered?"

"It was, my lord the earl," said Richard. "I may say to thee it was timely."

"Knowing from him what it was," said the earl, "I need ask no more on that head"; but he went on with what seemed to be only general inquiries as to the health of the archbishop and the gatherings of levies at York and elsewhere.

"Haste!" muttered Harcourt.

"On, then!" almost shouted the earl. "Ride well, thou of Wartmont, lest the foes of the Neville as well as the traitors to the king shall bar thy way. But I am glad that they lied who said that the good archbishop is failing. On!"

Silent and motionless upon their horses sat the men-at-arms as Harcourt and Richard galloped by.

7

Miles away, upon another road, a somewhat
like band of warlike men were halted as if wait·
ing, and to him who seemed their leader it was
said, by a small, gray-headed man at his side :

"Could we but know the mind of the arch·
bishop we might be able to tell the king why we
pay not his contributions, and why thy retainers
are not on the march for Portsmouth."

"We shall have his Grace's letters before the
sun is down," hoarsely responded the knight ad·
dressed. "I would there might be somewhat in
Wartmont's doublet to imperil the proud head of
his uncle Warwick."

"Aye, my Lord of Surrey," said the gray·
headed man, "it were overcunning of John Beau·
champ to have the young Neville so near the
prince. That house towereth too high. We will
tumble it somewhat."

Small was the knowledge of Richard concern·
ing the plots and perils through which he and his
had ridden, but in a small, elegantly furnished
room, at many a long mile's distance, there sat at
that hour twain who spoke of him.

"My son," remarked one of them, "I will not
say that thou and Warwick were overconfident to
send a boy. The time for his return draweth
near."

"'Tis far to ride," replied the younger of the
pair, and he was very much the younger. "I sent

Sir Geoffrey Harcourt to watch for him, else he might not come. My royal sire, Richard Neville and his archers might come and go where a knight and a score of men-at-arms would fail."

"Or turn traitor, as some have done," slowly responded the king. "The land reeks with treason, but half of it would have us go to France and be beaten, while the other half would have us stay at home and lose all to Philip of Valois."

So communed King Edward and the Black Prince, telling of the dangers which may beset a crown. Much had they to say concerning the power of the barons, but more of the building up of their strength among the people.

"Mark thou this, my son," said the king at last, "make thou the commons to be strong, and the crown is safe against the barons. When I can show thee bowmen defeating knights and men-at-arms, thou wilt see a new day for England. After that it shall not be long until a successful merchant shall be greater than an earl. Am not I also a merchant? Learn thou the art of the trader, for it is part of the wisdom of kings in the time that is coming."

All through his reign had commerce grown, and manufactures been encouraged by the king, while more and more with a strong hand he strove to restrain the barons. Not till a later day, however, were they to be broken; but, even as he now said, they were to go down partly by their own jealousies and feuds, but more by the power of the commons.

It was therefore a lesson in kingcraft that the prince was receiving from his father, but at the end of it the youth walked out along a corridor, murmuring:

"The king is sore disturbed. He hath great need to hear from York and of Scotland. Well for Richard Neville if he arrive speedily, for my royal father is not always safe in his mood. But he was pleased concerning the Neville and his archers."

It was sunset when Richard and Sir Geoffrey drew rein before a hostelry in a large hamlet.

"Dismount!" said the knight sharply. "I will give thee here a fresh horse, and thine shall follow. Ten leagues farther on, as I will give thee instruction, thou wilt get thee another. Ride till thou drop from thy saddle, but I trust thy toughness will bear thee through. If thou must sleep one night, camp thee in a wood, not in a house, lest thou awake and find thy pouch missing, or lest thou wake not at all."

The fresh horse was a good one, but now Richard, with full directions for the way, rode on alone, bearing still the banneret of the prince.

'Twas a fair night, and the full moon gave light as of the day. Mile after mile went by and all was well, but he came to an open level of broad highway whereon much could be seen afar.

"A man-at-arms?" said Richard. "He faceth this way. I may not let him stop me. I will close my visor and be ready for what may come."

He shut his helmet tightly and lowered his lance, loosening also the battle-axe at his saddle bow. He had need, for the strange man-at-arms uttered no warning, but dashed suddenly forward with lance in rest. 'Twas but the fortune of tourney, for the foeman rode well and he was large. His lance point glanced from the helmet of the young messenger, while Richard smote him full upon the breast.

Splintered to the hand was the lance, but the stranger reeled in the saddle, and before he could recover himself Richard had wheeled, axe in hand.

"In the king's name!" he shouted, "what doest thou with the king's messenger?"

Down came the battle-axe, striking the bridle arm of the stranger, so that while he drew his sword with his right hand he could not manage his horse.

"For the king!" shouted Richard.

"Down with thee, thou cub of Wartmont!" roared the stranger angrily. "I will take thy messages. Ha!"

'Twas a good blow, but it stopped upon the shield of the Neville, while once more the axe fell heavily with the curvet of Richard's horse. Sore wounded upon one thigh was now the man-at-arms, and his steed plunged viciously to one side.

"I will have thee!" he shouted, but his sword swept vainly through the air, while Richard charged again.

"Thy helm this time!" he muttered as his axe came down.

Cloven through was the steel headpiece, and the man-at-arms let fall his sword.

"Neville, I yield me!" he cried out. "Smite not again."

"Who art thou?" demanded Richard.

"That ask thou not, if thou art wise," responded the stranger. "For thee to know my name were thy death-warrant. Thou hast perils enough. Ride on, and tell the king that an old man-at-arms who could grind thee to powder hath been beaten by a lad. I have fought in twenty pitched fields, and now I must even ride home to save my broken head."

"I will harm thee not," said Richard, "but I fear thee not. Thy head were worth but little——"

"Trust me, it is safe," said the stranger. "The king will leave it where it is. I shall see thee again some day. Thou wilt be a good lance, but carry thou not too many king's errands. Fare thee well!"

He had regained control of his horse, and now

he suddenly spurred away in the very direction by which Richard had come. Down sprang the latter to pick up the fallen lance and to fasten upon it the pennon his own had carried before it was broken. Then, as he mounted once more, he exclaimed aloud :

"Ride I now for my life! I shall be followed fast and far. I know not friend from foe, save that the nearer I get to the king the safer I shall be."

His good horse neighed cheerily, as if he knew that his rider had conquered, and a proud youth was Richard Neville.

"I have won my first passage at arms," he said. "I shall have somewhat whereof to tell the prince."

CHAPTER V.

"SEVEN leagues from London, if that wagoner gave me the distance aright," said Richard to himself, "and this horse is sore wearied. Twain have tired under me since my lance was splintered on the shield of that felon knight."

Much and often had he wondered who might be the stranger man-at-arms, but of one thing he felt assured : only some baron of high name had used such speech and worn such armor. Now, at last, even his tough sinews were giving out, for he had ridden hard and slept little. Food had been easy to buy at wayside hostelries. He had ridden through towns and villages with no longer pauses than had been needful that he might ask the way or answer courteously the questions of persons of condition.

His fresh mounts had been freely furnished him on showing of the royal order, for none might lightly disobey the king.

"Surely I now am safe," he thought, "but the

96

night is falling. I will even rest at an inn and go onward in the morning. I must sleep, lest I fall from my horse."

It was a huge, rambling tavern at the right of the highway, and as he drew rein before it a portly host came forth to welcome him.

"In the king's name," said Richard.

"And whence art thou?" asked the landlord.

"On the king's business," said Richard. "See thou to it that I have a fresh steed ready to bear me to London town with the dawn, lest harm come."

"We are all the king's men here," said the land-lord heartily. "Canst thou not give us the news of the day? What of the Scots? for thou art from the north."

Richard was slowly, painfully dismounting, but at the same moment another man, not in armor, was springing upon horseback to haste away.

"Yea," said Richard, "I will tell thee the news. I am Richard Neville of Wartmont——"

"Ha! hold thou thy tongue, then, and come in!" sharply returned the host of the inn, but he spoke in pure Saxon. "Do I not know that thou art watched for? I am of Arden, and I knew thy father. By thy hand fell the Club of Devon."

"Aye," said Richard, "but what peril is so near the gates of London?"

"Peril to thee that thou reach them not," replied his new friend. "There be those who would know the king's secret counsel. Small would be their care for thy throat. Eat well. Sleep well. Then ride thou on before the light cometh."

In walked Richard, hardly able to stand, but a room was given him, and here he took off his armor that he might bathe while a repast was preparing. It refreshed him much, but when the landlord came in and found him clad only in his doublet, he loudly exclaimed:

"On with thy mail, my Lord of Wartmont! Let thy bare sword lie by thee. I think thy nag may die, but I have thee a better one ready. 'Tis my own best mare, and she will stand saddled in the stall until thou comest for her."

"I am overworn for fighting," said Richard. "I will even trust my bow rather than my sword or axe."

"As thou wilt," replied his host, but a serving man placed food upon the table, and Richard began to do it full justice.

None other was admitted to the room, and Richard dealt fairly, telling all news that he might tell.

"One thing know I," said the landlord. "The king's levies come in but slowly, and he is sore displeased. Not this year will he cross to France. If I hear truly, some of the great lords would rather march against him than against Philip, and they look for side help from the Scots."

So many true tales creep in at a hostel from the lips of those who tarry there, and the young messenger felt not only weary but half dispirited. The landlord had now gone forth, and for a few moments Richard was alone. The door was not fastened, however, and it opened without a sound to let in a man whose footsteps were unheard until he had passed to the table side.

"My son, peace be with thee! Thou art on the message of the king?"

Richard was startled, but he turned to look, and before him stood a black friar in his long serge robe, with sandals only on his feet. A thought came like a flash:

"I have heard that these holy men are with Philip of France rather than with Edward of England. I must beware of him, for they are cunning men."

Nevertheless he reverently greeted the friar and bade him be seated.

"Tell me, my son, what tidings bringest thou from the north, and from the saintly Archbishop of York?"

With all seeming freedom did Richard respond, but he mentioned not the Knight of Liddesdale, nor the temper of the Scottish king. Cunning indeed was the questioning, but of the letters, either way, naught was said. Rather was there much loose chat of the things by the way, and Richard declared :

"Little know I. I am but a youth."

"And well worn ?" said the monk. "Now I will counsel thee, for thou well mayest trust such as I am. Rest thou here in peace, and I will convey to the king any matters from my old and dear friend and father in God, the archbishop. High, indeed, is my reverence for that holy man. Deep is my fealty to our good lord the king. Even give me thy message and I will depart."

"Thanks to thee, reverend father," said Richard. "But there is no haste. It were not well for thee to travel by night. Come thou in the morning, for now I can talk no more. Thou mayest ride my own horse, if thou shalt find him rested."

So the friar smiled, and gave Richard his blessing and departed, not having given any name. That was what came to Richard's mind quickly, but he said to himself :

"Who knoweth what name he would have given—his own, or another ? I like him not, but if the host be right, he will not ride far upon that nag. Nor will he be overweighted with the king's errand. But I told him no untruth. Never before was I cunning, but I must care for my head."

So said the landlord, shortly, when he came and heard, but he added :

"Not in the house shalt thou sleep. Come thou with me, my lord. I will show thee a safer resting."

The darkness had fallen, and not even a lanthorn did they take with them as they made their way out of the inn to the barns. None met them, and they paused not until they were among hayricks in the rear.

"Yonder," said the landlord, pointing at a stable, "in the first stall on the right is thy good steed. Ride hard, but kill her not, and send her back to me. I would serve the king and beat his enemies. If thou sleepest too long, I will arouse thee."

Down sank Richard upon a heap of hay, but his bow and arrows were with him as well as his pennoned lance.

How long he slumbered he knew not, but he was feverish, restive, and his ears were not so dull in sleep that they did not catch a faint clang of steel. He woke, but he stirred not, and he lay listening.

"Put thou thy dagger deeply in below the lad's ear!" he heard one say. "He must die without speech. Curse on that hostel keeper! I fear me he hath betrayed us. We found not the king's messenger in the house. I think he is somewhere here away. Search well, but be silent."

Only dim was the lanthorn they carried, but

Richard could see three men, and one of them wore mail, without a headpiece. He it was that spoke, and his sword was in his hand. The other twain were in buff coats, and of one of these his long, two-edged, dagger knife was already drawn. They saw not yet the young bowman in the hay, but he was fitting an arrow to the string.

"Ten yards! I must not miss. I will even smite him through the face," thought Richard.

Loudly twanged the bow, and out of the belt came a second arrow to the string.

"Through his buff coat," said Richard aloud, and he sent the shaft strongly, but he at the moment turned toward the stable, looking not behind him. He heard a cry and a gasp, however, and hoarse groaning, and a voice that exclaimed:

"God 'a' mercy, my Lord Bellamont is slain! So is the seneschal! Woe is me! I will summon the two warders."

Uncertainly he lingered a brief space to examine well the fallen men, and Richard made what haste he could.

"I can not run," he thought. "I hardly may climb to the saddle."

Nevertheless he did so, after leading out the goodly beast he was to ride. Nothing was lacking in her appointments, and she knew the way to the road-gate. Out spurred Richard, as loud shouts began to arise behind him. He gained the high-

Loudly twanged the bow.

way, and he could discern beyond him only one man on foot, in full armor.

"Halt, thou!" he shouted. "Stand, on thy life! I would have speech with thee!"

"In the king's name," shouted back Richard, "out of my way!"

"That will I not!" roared the knight. "Thou cub of Wartmont, draw rein!"

"Take that!" said Richard, spurring hard and striking with his lance.

'Twas a knight of skill in fence, however, and his target was over his visor to receive the thrust, so that he did but measure his length upon the road.

"Traitor!" shouted Richard. "Thou shalt answer for this to the king!"

"St. Andrew!" gasped the fallen man. "Has the boy escaped? John Beauchamp knew whom to send. But I will pay him bitterly for this."

"My lord duke," exclaimed one who came running to him, "De Bellamont is slain by the messenger!"

"Woe worth the day!" groaned the knight, arising slowly. "Back to the castle! I must get me to Flanders in haste. All is lost! We will but say that Bellamont was murdered by thieves at the inn."

On galloped Richard, glad to find how buoyant and free was the stride of the landlord's favorite;

but his perils were not ended. A full half mile he rode, and he was thinking, " I will race no more lest I tire her needlessly, and the road to London town is yet long," when far beyond he dimly discerned the forms of mounted men and men on foot.

" 'Tis but a lane here to the right," he said. "I care not whither it may lead me, so I fall not in with yonder troop. They are too many."

Then came to him something of his woodcraft, and he did but go out of the road before he turned to see what they might do. And he did wisely, for with one accord the horsemen and the footmen vanished.

" They were at a crossroad," thought Richard. " They deem I have taken the lane, and they have gone to cut me off at its ending. Now I will ride past them."

'Twas a shrewd planning, for when he reached the crossroads only one man could he discern, a man in the serge gown of a black friar, who stood and waited.

"Halt, thou, my son!" commanded the friar. " Greater men than thou art bid thee stand."

" In the king's name, I will not," said Richard, " but if thou needest a nag, thou wilt find one at the inn, as I promised thee. A good beast, truly, save that he is dead. So are some of the traitors who were there, enemies of the king, as thou art. Fare thee not well!"

He struck spurs as he finished, and the friar was left to wait for whom he might.

The gray dawn was showing in the east, and now it would seem that all danger had been left behind.

"Little know I," thought Richard. "Had I not been forewarned, I had trusted any great baron that he would forward the king's business. Now I will trust not one, till I reach London gate."

The noon sun of that day was shining through high, stained windows into the audience chamber of the king, in the Tower of London. It was not a day for him to linger in any palace, and his brows were but black with gloom as he listened to his counselors and to the affairs that were brought before him. These were many and weighty, and few were they who might dare to interrupt him; but he suddenly raised his head, and the dark frown vanished from his face.

Back among the lords and gentlemen in waiting stood the Black Prince himself, and a sign had passed from him to his royal sire. Still for a few moments longer King Edward sat and listened and responded to those around him, nor could they have gathered whether he were ill at ease or not. Iron was he to all circumstances, and naught could seem to move him much, save his ire, if that should be stirred.

And now he arose, and his dismissal of the as-
8

sembly was but as if he sent them to their noontide refections, but he himself refused other at-
tendance, and passed out by a private door with
his son.

"Neville of Wartmont, from the archbishop?"
sternly replied the king to the first words of the
prince. "Why tarried he on the road?"

"That he did not," said the prince. "He hath
ridden four horses. One wearied out, twain were
ridden to death, and the last bore him to our gate.
He hath been sore beset on the way. He hath
slain De Bellamont and another, and he hath much
to tell concerning treason. I bade him wait in the
southerly corridor and to have speech with none."

"It shall be well with him!" exclaimed the
king. "Glad am I of the Nevilles and the Beauchamps in a day when so few may be trusted.
Bring him to me in my retiring room."

Unhelmeted, but otherwise clad as he had ridden, Richard Neville was quietly conducted to the
apartment which so few were ever allowed to enter, and he was brought face to face with the king.

"Nay, Richard, sit thee down," commanded
Edward, for the wornout messenger hardly could
rise from his bended knees. "I would hear thee
slowly and long. Begin with thy going, and see
that thou miss no place nor any man, gentle or
simple."

Richard began his tale, and there was no interruption until he came to the message sent by the Earl of Arundel.

"I will remember him for that," he said. "A wise man and true. Speak on."

There was no other stopping until the story reached the York gate.

"Sir Robert," said the king, "then I may trust the Johnstones. It is well. Come now to the archbishop. Nay, hold thy letters until thy words are done."

There were questions concerning his Grace and some others, but most careful were the king's inquiries relating to the Knight of Liddesdale.

"Now, thy ride hitherward," said the king, and Richard told it all. He saw the eyes of the prince flash admiringly at the passage of arms, but the king chafed sorely that he could not guess by whom Richard had been assailed.

"Thou didst well not to slay him," he decided, after a moment's thinking. "If thou ever meetest him again, to know him by his voice or otherwise, tell me."

When all the rest was said, to the London gate, the letters were delivered, but the king as yet opened them not.

"Richard of Wartmont," he said, rising, "the Earl of Warwick waiteth for thee without. Go thou to him. God send me alway as good a messenger! Thou wilt win thy spurs in good season.

When thou returnest from Warwick, thou art of the king's household. I promise thee that thou shalt be captain of thine own bowmen when we sail for France."

A proud youth was Richard, but so lame he walked not easily when the prince led him to the door.

"I envy thee, I envy thee!" exclaimed the latter. "A joust of arms by moonlight! A fray i' the night! And thou hast seen the Liddesdale! I would give much to meet him."

Something of romance and of knight errantry, therefore, was in the hot young head of the heir of the throne of England, and they twain parted right friendly, as became such youths, who were to be companions in arms.

In one moment more, upon Richard's shoulders were the strong hands of the Earl of Warwick.

"Thou art as my son!" he exclaimed. "Thou art strengthening thy house. These be times when a man should stand by his own."

Few were the words of their further greeting till they were by themselves in the Warwick palace at London. Nor then was much converse, until Richard had slept long and well. Afterward he was talked with by his uncle as if he had been a grown man and a belted knight, but that was on the morrow.

"Moreover," said the earl, at the end of all,

"I have thy freedom from the king. Thou mayest pause in Warwick to see thy mother. Then
go thou to Wartmont. Spend what time thou
mayest among thy men, but be sure that thy levy
shall be full. So shalt thou keep the favor of the
king. Then thou wilt return to London town."

One day only was required, and beyond that
was the homeward road. Oh, but it was a bright
even, full of happiness, when the young warrior—
for such he now was—once more was folded in
the arms of the Lady Maud! Her long, white
hair fell over his shoulders like a veil, and she
sobbed most peacefully.

"Alas, my son," she said, "that I can not keep
thee with me! Thou art mine all! But obey
thou the mandates of the king and of the earl."

"I must speed me to Wartmont, mother," said
Richard. "I will return to thee, but it will please
me much to see the old tower again, and my merry
men."

There were two sunsets after that before he
left the castle, and proud was she at the manner
of his treatment by the great men who were coming and going. Any were ready to speak graciously to a youth who was known to have won
royal favor.

Only the third sun was going down thereafter,
when Richard, in full armor but alone, save a
serving man with a pack beast heavily laden, drew

rein before the portal of his own castle. But all behind him the village had risen as he rode through. Farmer men were also coming in, while every cottage poured forth old and young.

The warders raised the portcullis and swung open the gate, while in the tower the bell swung heels over head. So in the village church the ringers were busy, to show their young lord their gladness at his safe return. For there had been rumors of his going to the north, even unto Scotland. He had slain men. He had served the king. He had done wondrous well, and all his own were joyful.

Hardly could he dismount from his good steed, so close was the press around him, but he bade the castle keepers make ready a goodly feast for all comers.

"Guy the Bow!" he shouted suddenly, "art thou here?"

Not quite had he arrived, but up the street a galloway was coming at his swiftest, and on his bare back rode the best archer of Arden. Down sprang Richard now, and so did Guy, but there was no handshaking, for Richard's arms were around the forester.

"Come thou within!" he shouted. "I have much to tell thee. Much to tell the men. How goeth it with them all?"

"Right well, my Lord Richard," said Guy,

greatly delighted. "I tell thee, they came back loyal men. A fortnight's gay drilling with the king's troops. Good fare. Wages as if in war. A now suit each. Then marched they home, avowing they would bring each his man to double the levy."

"I trust they may," said Richard. "I will have speech with them."

"But seest thou not," said Guy, "what the earl's masons are doing for thy castle? I wonder at it, for the time hath been but brief. They work fast, and the walls are nobly mended."

"I will see to that," said Richard eagerly, and they pushed on into the keep, but not till he had spoken many good words to the villagers. Truly the workmen had plied their tools with industry, but they had done more than mend. Some well-skilled engineer of the earl had planned enlarge-ments and outer walls on the farther side. There were to be bastions and stronger battlements and better storage within for the provenders that might withstand a siege. It was a good fort, had said the engineer, and in some dark day it might be worth the holding.

That evening was a feast of welcome and of news-telling, but with the dawn both Guy and Richard rode away. Nor did any at the castle know whither they had gone nor what they did while they were away. All the while the masons and their helpers toiled on, and the stonework grew

apace.   It was four days before the young lord of
Wartmont returned to see what they had done.
A score of men on galloways came with him to the
edge of the forest, but there they drew rein, and it
was Ben of Coventry who spoke for them.

"Fare thee well, Lord Richard of Wartmont!"
he said merrily.   "We will come at the king's
summons, hear it when we may.   Only this, that
thou do not get thyself slain too soon, for many of
us will follow the Neville, and not another."

If he had won them, so had they won him, and
well did he love his bowmen, as one loveth kith
and kin.

Not long might be his further lingering at the
castle nor on the road to Warwick.   There, indeed, he found not only his mother, but a message
from the earl, bidding him to London speedily.
It was a grief, and yet she was willing to have him
go, for in it was his future good fortune, and she
kissed him farewell after a long talk about Wartmont, and the grange in the forest, and the troop
he was to command, although so young.

Two mounted spearmen went with him on the
road to London, but none who met him questioned
him for harm.   It was as if the roads were as safe
and peaceful as was their seeming; but Richard
knew better than that.   Even at the London gate
he found himself turning quickly in his saddle to
gaze after one who passed him.

" 'Twas a scowling face," he thought. " Where have I met that knight? He carrieth his bridle arm in a sling, as if he were wounded there. Did I not smite a left arm with mine axe on the road? I will watch for that man."

So he told the prince when they came together, but there was wisdom of kingcraft in the answer given.

"O true and loyal heart, good comrade," spoke the prince, "if thou thinkest thou knowest him, be sure that thou know him not. If he meet thee, greet him well, as if he were thy kinsman. 'Tis ever well for a man to know his foemen. 'Tis ever ill to let his foemen know that he knoweth them. Safety is in secrecy until the sword is out of the sheath."

"I will obey," said Richard, "but my blade will be out quickly if any seem to threaten thee or my royal master."

The prince inquired with care concerning the archery levy, and he seemed well pleased, but he had somewhat more of counsel for his companion in arms.

"Wert thou ever on shipboard?" he asked. "Hast thou been ever at sea?"

"Never saw I the salt water," responded Richard. "I have but looked upon the masts in the Thames, but I can row a boat."

"A wherry?" said the prince. "There will be

no wherry fighting. Even now we are sweeping the French pirate craft from the Channel. Do thou this: at every hour of thy liberties haunt thou the riverside. Read thou each craft thou seest, great and small. I will get thee an order to board any in the king's errand. Talk with seafaring men, and learn the points of shipping and of the manner of all fights at sea. Go not out of the harbor, however, for thou mayest not at any day be beyond recall if thou art needed as a messenger. Thou art of the king's pages. The earl will see to thy equipment, for thou mayest often serve at court and at royal banquets."

Gladly did he hear of that appointment. None of lower rank than his own might carry a dish or hand a napkin at the royal table, or stand behind any of the king's guests in the banquet hall. But hardly less than an earl might deliver the king's own cup or carve or hand for him.

Much teaching of these matters did Richard receive thereafter from the Earl of Warwick, and likewise one of his near friends and tutors was the good Earl of Arundel, brave knight and skillful captain, fitted to lead an army. Noble ladies also smiled upon him, for he was well favored and of goodly stature, and he knew somewhat of music. Even the queen herself spoke graciously to him before long. Nevertheless did he walk always cautiously, knowing more and more of the bitter jealousies and heartburnings which ever beset a court, and of the feuds of houses, and of the plots and cunnings, and of the endless rivalries for place and power and the favor of the king.

Long hours were to be spent each day in the hall of arms of the Warwick palace. There were duties of drill and exercise among the soldiery, that he might know how to work maneuverings on a field or placings on a march, or the choosing and the putting in order of a camp. He learned also of forts and of defenses, and of attacks and of artful dealings with foemen by night or day.

"I will make thee fitted to command thy men," said Earl Warwick. "Thou shalt not go into battle untrained. We learn that Philip of France is taking no such pains with his musterings. He will trust to his counts and barons and to his allies. He will bring against us a multitude, and then he will see what Edward of England will do with his motley array."

Greater and greater grew Richard's confidence, like that of other men, in the war wisdom of his king, but he marveled much from time to time at the words and the deep thinking of his friend the prince. He could speak several tongues, and prudently, and he was notable for his feats of skill and strength in the royal hall of arms.

It was not at first that Richard had leisure to learn much of the sea, save in listening to the talk

of knights and captains who had served on shipboard. But he forgot not the counsel of the
prince, and in due season he was busy with his new
learning.

"Hard work," he said at the beginning. "Even
the ropes have names, and every rope hath a place
of its own. So have the spars and the sails. 'Tis
another tongue to win, and the sailors are not like
our inland men. They believe, too, that a man who
liveth not on the sea is of small account. They
have more respect for a good sailor than for a lord,
if so be his lordship knoweth not how to win a
sea fight. But they believe that our king is an admiral. What pirates they are in their talk! I
have met no sailor yet who thinketh it ill to capture and plunder any foreign craft that he may en-
counter out of sight of land."

That was the fashion of those times, for all the
open seas were as disputed territory, and the best
sailors of those waters adjacent to the coasts of the
British isles were but as the grandsons of the vikings. Not at all as yet had they abandoned the
wild traditions of their roving ancestors.

Ever and anon came tidings from the north
counties, but such as came to the public ear were
favorable to a continued peace with Scotland;
only that all men knew that a Scottish peace was
only a war asleep, and was to be kept with the
English sword halfway out of the scabbard.

From the Continent of Europe came no peace at all, but from every quarter was heard the clash of arms or the sound of military preparation. Embassies came and went continually, and Richard saw many men whose names were of note in the lands beyond the sea. He studied them well, and he inquired as he might of their deeds in camp and field and council, but none did he see who seemed to him the equals of his own great captains.

Slowly wore on the winter, and the spring went by. His mother came to court with the Countess of Warwick, and Richard was proud to see her in the throne room, unsurpassed by any dame therein for her stately beauty of form and face, and for the sweet graciousness with which she greeted all.

'Twas a fine, fair morn in June when Richard at last was summoned in haste by the Earl of Warwick.

"Grand news, my young kinsman!" shouted the stout earl. "The die is cast! The war with France hath come! Be thou ready!"

"Ready am I," said Richard gladly. "But I must bring my bowmen with me."

"Go thou not, then," said the earl. "Send but thy token by thy own messengers. Bid all the archers of Arden to speed them to Portsmouth in the king's name. The ships are even now gathering rapidly. Thousands of men are in perfect training, and the new levies are in hand to learn

the way and the will of the king. Thither wilt
thou go thyself. Bid thy mother a long farewell,
and haste thee. I trust that when thou seest her
again thou wilt wear golden spurs."

"Please God," said Richard, "I will strive to
earn the good will of the king. I would not be
knighted by any lesser hand than his. Canst thou
tell me where is my noble friend Sir Walter de
Maunay ? "

"Somewhere in Guienne," said the earl, "and
the king's enemies there may roundly will that he
were somewhere else. Now up and out, Richard
Neville ! Thou wilt get thy orders further from
Geoffrey Harcourt, at the port. I go to Warwick
first, and then I come. The days of this mock
peace are ended, and may God give his blessing to
the armies of England and to our good lord the
king ! Amen."

CHAPTER VI.

"Thou art no seaman!" laughed the prince. "I think thou wouldst learn to love the sea, as do all true English hearts. Go thou on board forthwith. The admiral hath given thee one Piers Fleming for thy shipmaster."

Profoundly respectful was the answer of Richard Neville, for his friend was also his prince and his commander; he said, " 'Tis but a brief passage, and there will be no fighting."

"Count not on that," replied the prince. "We are warned of many French rovers, from Calais and elsewhere, on the watch for stragglers. Word cometh that the king is safely at La Hogue, in Normandy, and not, as some think, in Guienne. There will soon be enough of fighting on land, but watch thou for a chance to gain honor on the sea. We must win our spurs before we return to Merry England."

The two young men, neither of them yet eighteen, were standing on the height above Portsmouth, gazing down upon the harbor and out upon the sea. In all directions there were swarms of vessels of all sizes, sailing or at anchor; for it was said that King Edward the Third had gathered over a thousand ships to convey his army across the Channel for his quarrel with Philip of France.

It was the largest English fleet yet assembled, and the army going on board was also the best with which any English king had ever put to sea. It consisted of picked men only. Of these, four thousand were men-at-arms, six thousand were Irish, twelve thousand were Welsh; but the most carefully trained and disciplined part of the force consisted of ten thousand bowmen. During a whole year had Edward and his son and his generals toiled to select and prepare the men and the weapons with which they were to meet the highly famed chivalry of the Continent. An army selected from a nation of perhaps four millions of people was to contend with an army collected from France with her twenty millions, and from such allies of hers as Germany and Bohemia, re-enforced by large numbers of paid mercenaries. Among these latter were the crossbowmen of Genoa sold to Philip by the masters of that Italian oligarchy. Edward's adventure had a seeming of great rashness, for already it was reported that the French king had mustered a hundred thousand men. Full many a gallant cavalier in armor of proof may well have wondered to hear, moreover, that Edward the Third, accounted the foremost general of his time, proposed to meet superior numbers of the best lances of Europe with lightly armored men on foot. They knew not yet of the new era that was dawning upon the science of war. Edward and his bowmen were to teach the world more than one new lesson before that memorable campaign was over. Before this, he had shown what deeds might be wrought upon the sea by ships prepared and manned and led by himself. He had so crippled the naval power of his enemies that there was now no hostile fleet strong enough to prevent his present undertaking, although Philip had managed to send out some scores of cruisers to do whatever harm they could.

The prince was clad in a full suit of the plain black armor from which his popular name had been given him. His visor was up, and his resolute, intelligent face wore a dignity beyond his years.

The stature of the young hero of England was nearly that of full-grown manhood ; and if Richard was not quite so tall, he was both older and stronger than when he had faced the Club of Devon in the village street of Wartmont.

A brilliant company of men-at-arms stood around them, many of whom were famous knights and mighty barons. Richard was now receiving his final instructions, and in a few minutes more he bowed low and departed.

9

Halfway down the hill he was awaited by a party of stalwart-looking men, and to one of these he said:

"Haste thee now, Guy the Bow! Let us have the sails up and get out of the harbor. Almost the entire army is already on board."

"Aye, my lord," responded the bowman; "I have been all over our ship. The sailors are good men and true; but I like not the captain, and we shall be crowded like sheep in a pen."

"'Tis but for a day," said Richard, "and the weather is good. We are warned of foes by the way."

"We shall be ready for them," said Guy; then he added, "A page from my Lord the Earl of War-wick brought this."

It was a letter, and quickly it came open.

"It is from my mother! The saints be with her!" exclaimed Richard. "She is well. I will read it fully after we are on board. Thanks to the good earl."

Down the hill they went together, and on to a long pier, at the outer end of which was moored a two-masted vessel apparently of about four hun-dred tons' burden—a large vessel for those days—very high at bow and stern, but low amidships, as if she were planned to carry a kind of wooden fort at each end.

She was ready to cast off as soon as the young

commander came on board ; and he was greeted by
loud cheers from her crowded decks.

"She is thronged to the full," said Richard.

The sailing-master stood before him. He was
a square-built man, of middle age, with a red face
and small, greenish-gray eyes. His beard and hair
were closely cropped and stiff; he wore a steel
body-coat and headpiece, but his feet were bare.
An unpleasant man to look upon was Piers Fleming; and behind him stood one not more than
half as old, but of the same pattern, so like he
needed not to say that he was the master's son, as
well as mate of the Golden Horn.

"The wind is fair, sir," said Fleming. "We go
out with the tide, but a fog is coming up the
Channel."

"Cast off," said Richard. "Yonder on the
height is the prince with his lords and gentlemen,
watching the going."

"Aye, aye!" responded Fleming. "He shall
see the Golden Horn go out."

She cleared the harbor in gallant style, with
her sails full spread, while Richard busied himself
among his men. The crew was thirty strong,
mostly Englishmen.

"I have but twenty men-at-arms," said Richard
to himself at the end of his inspection, "but there
are two hundred and more of bowmen, and over a
hundred Irish pikemen, besides the Welshmen.

What bones those Irish are made with! I will
serve out axes among them without delay. Fine
chopping should be done by such brawny axemen
as they."

"Richard Neville," whispered an eager voice at
his elbow, "I pray thee hearken. One of the sailors, a Londoner, understandeth Flemish. He hath
heard the captain and his son have speech with
one on the pier. There is treason afoot, my Lord.
Watch thou, and I will pass the word among the
men."

"Tell all," said Richard, with a hot flush on
his face; but there was little enough to tell. It
could be but a warning, a cause for suspicion and
for care.

"Guy the Bow," said Richard, at the end of
their brief talk, "seek among the sailors for a true
Englishman fit to take the helm if I smite off the
head of this Piers Fleming. Let thy man keep near
me if a foe appeareth."

Yet stronger blew the south wind, and, as Piers
had said, with it came a thick, bluish mist that
hid the ships from one another and made it impossible for any landsman on board of them to more
than guess in what direction he might be going.
It was therefore not thought of by Richard as of
any importance that the Golden Horn was speeding
full before the wind. She was going northerly, instead of taking a tack toward La Hogue. Right

with her blew the mist, and hour after hour went by. Several times hoarse hails were heard and answered, but all were in the hearty voices of loyal Englishmen, and Richard said to one of his men-at-arms:

"We are with the fleet, and all is well."

Most of them had put aside their armor, as being too heavy to wear needlessly during so sultry a day; for it was the 2d of July, 1346, and the summer was a warm one; the bowmen and pike-men also had taken off their heavy buff coats and laid aside their arms.

But among the groups passed some of Richard's Longwood archers, talking low; and all the while, without attracting attention, sheaves of arrows, extra spears, with poleaxes and battle-axes and shields, were being handed up from the store of weapons in the hold.

Piers Fleming was at the helm, and near him stood his son. There were grim smiles on their faces while they glanced up at the rigging and out into the mist, and noted the compass and the direction of the wind.

"Son Hans," at last muttered the old man, "it can not be long now. Some of the Calais craft are sure to be hereabout. We will lay this tubful of English pirates alongside right speedily, if so be it is a large ship of good strength."

"They will be caught napping," growled Hans.

"'Twill be a fine prize, for the hold is packed to tightness."

" Well bloweth the wind," said Piers, "and the Golden Horn hath now no company."

At the forward end of the low waist of the ship stood Richard among his men.

" Ye do know well," he said, "and all must know, that they would show no quarter. Every man fighteth for his life, for who is taken goeth overboard, dead or alive."

" Aye," responded Ben o' Coventry; " 'tis a cut-throat business. I think there would be small room for any Frenchman on the Golden Horn, if one should come aboard."

"Room enough in the sea," said the red-haired O'Rourke, who was captain of the Irish; and he turned then to talk to his gigantic kerns in their own tongue. So did a man named David Griffith talk to a throng of broad-shouldered Welshmen who were also on board, armed with short swords, daggers, and spears or darts. Of the latter several bundles now lay amidships.

Back toward the stern strode Richard slowly, and after him, as if they were drifting about without special intention, strolled three rugged-looking seamen from the old port of London.

The waves ran not too high for a gay summer cruise, and the Golden Horn rode them steadily. She was a fast sailer, for all her breadth of beam.

Suddenly her course was changed, and her sails swung in a little; for a command from Captain Fleming sent men to haul on the sheets. Just then a long-drawn vibrating whistle had been heard, and it sounded thrice, from the very direction the ship was taking.

Richard stood now on the high after-deck, and a wave of his hand could be seen by his men below. There was little apparent stir among them, but buff coats were quickly donned, bows were strung, sheaves of arrows were cut open and distributed, while the men-at-arms made ready, and the Irish made sure of their grip upon pikes and axes.

"We will speak that ship, my Lord Neville," said Fleming, very respectfully. "I have orders to report all craft we meet at sea."

"Aye, speak to her," said Richard; but he loosened his sword in its sheath, and he knew that Guy the Bow had an arrow on the string.

Loudly came a hail from out of the fog; the speaker was a Frenchman, and hardly had his utterance ceased before it was followed by a tumult of fierce, triumphant cheering on board the strange vessel.

Piers Fleming sent back a hoarse reply, speaking French; and then he turned to Richard.

"She cometh, my lord!" he exclaimed, as if much affrighted. "'Tis one of King Philip's

great cruisers. I have bidden them that we surrender."

He was steering straight for the huge vessel
which now swept toward them, looking larger
through the cloud of vapor; but ere he made reply Richard's sword was drawn.

"Thou art a traitor!" he shouted. "Jack of
London, take thou the helm!"

"Never!" cried Fleming. "Resistance were
madness! We are almost alongside of her. Ho,
Monsieur de Gaines! We surrender!"

Richard's sword flashed like lightning, but even
before it fell had sped the arrow of Guy the Bow.
The strong hands of the ready English mariner
caught the tiller as the traitorous sailing-master
fell gasping to the deck. His son Hans had been
standing hard by him, pike in hand. He was taken
by surprise for a moment, but he made a quick
thrust at Richard. There had been deadly peril
in that thrust, but that a poleaxe in the hand of an
Irishman came down and cleft the traitor to the
eyes.

The great French ship came on majestically,
but Richard had given careful orders beforehand,
and the Golden Horn did not avoid closing with
her.

"Let them board us," he had said, and Ben o'
Coventry had replied to him: "Aye, my Lord
'o Wartmont, and we will slay as many as we

may upon our own decks before we finish upon theirs."

So little thought had the English but that they should win, no matter who came.

Louder and louder now arose the exulting yells and shouts from the swarms of armed men surging to and fro upon the fore and after forts and in the waist of La Belle Calaise, as her grapnels were thrown out to fasten upon the Golden Horn. She was much the taller and larger vessel, and even her tops and rigging were full of men.

Alas for these! Had they been so many squirrels in the trees of Longwood, they could not have dropped faster as the English archers plied their deadly bows. Of the latter, too, some were in the cuplike tops of the Golden Horn, and their shafts were seeking marks among the French knights and men-at-arms. It was a fearful moment, for the boarders were ready as the two ships crashed against each other.

"Steady, men! Stand fast!" shouted Richard. "Let them come on, but slay them as they come! Take the knights first; aim at the armholes. Waste no shaft. St. George for merry England! For the king and for the prince!"

"For the king and for Richard of Wartmont!" shouted Ben o' Coventry.

Twang went his bow as he spoke, and a tall knight in full armor pitched heavily forward upon the deck of the Golden Horn, shouting "St. Denis!" as he fell. His sword had been lifted, and the gray goose shaft had taken him in the arm-pit. He would strike no more.

The Frenchmen were brave enough, and they did not seem to be dismayed even by the dire carnage which was thinning them out so rapidly. The worst thing against them was that all this was so entirely unexpected. They had counted upon taking the English ship by surprise, aided by the treachery of Piers Fleming and his son. The Golden Horn had been steered by them many a long mile out of her proper course, and the same trick may have been played upon others of King Edward's transports; for he had been compelled to employ sailors of all the nationalities along the Channel and the North Sea, excepting a few that favored the Frenchmen.

The fighting force on La Belle Calaise was not only double the number of that on the Golden Horn, but it contained five times as many men-at-arms. There the advantage ended, however; for the rest of it consisted of a motley mob of all sorts, woefully inferior in arms, discipline, and even in bodily strength to the chosen fighters who were commanded by Richard of Wartmont.

For a few minutes he had kept his post on the high deck at the stern, that he might better see how the fight was going. Then, however, with his score of men in full armor, he went down in the waist, stepping forward to meet the onset of the French knights who dashed in to avenge their fallen leader. He had not been their only commander, evidently, for now in their front there stood a knight whose splendid arms and jeweled crest marked him as a noble of high rank.

"God and St. Denis!" he shouted. "Down with the dogs of England!"

"St. George and King Edward! I am Richard Neville of Wartmont. Who art thou?"

Their swords were crossing as the Frenchman responded, "Antoine, Count de Renly! Down with thee, thou of Wartmont! I will give an account of thee to thy boy Black Prince."

"I am another boy, as he is," was the reply from the young lord; for his antagonist was certainly not taller than himself, and they were not badly matched.

All around them the fierce *mêlée* went on. Arrows whizzed; the spears of the Welshmen flew; there was hard hammering of sword and axe on helm and shield. One fact came out which men of knightly degree might otherwise have doubted. It was seen that a strong Irishman, with only his buff coat for armor or for weight, could swing a weapon more freely and with better effect than could a brave knight a head shorter, of lighter bones, weighed down by armor of proof and a steel-faced shield. Fierce was the wild Irish war-cry with which these brawny men of Ulster and Connaught rushed forward, and their swinging blows were as the stroke of death. Shields were dashed aside, helmets and mail were cloven through. Slain they were, a number of them; but they had not fallen uselessly—there were not now so many Frenchmen in full armor.

Richard and De Renly were skilled swordsmen, and for a time neither of them seemed able to gain any advantage. The Frenchman was a knight of renown, however, and it angered him to be checked by a mere youngster, a boy, a squire only, from the household of the Black Prince. He lost his tem-per, and pushed forward rashly, forgetting that he was not now upon firm land. The wind still blew, and the waves were lifting the ships, grinding them one against the other with shocks that were stag-gering. There was blood upon the deck at the spot where the mailed foot of the count was pressed. He slipped as he struck, and the sword of the English boy smote hard upon his crest.

A rush, another slip, another blow, and De Renly lay upon the deck, with the point of Rich-ard's blade at the bars of his helmet.

" Yield thee, De Renly ! " he shouted, " rescue or no rescue. Yield, or thou diest ! "

" I yield ! " came hoarsely back; " but myself only, not my ship."

"Yield thee, De Renly!" he shouted.

"Yield thee!" said Richard, taking away his sword. "We will care for thy boat."

Loudly laughed the O'Rourke at Neville's triumph; and he smote down a man-at-arms right across the fallen De Renly.

"Hout, my Lord of Wartmont!" he shouted. "Thou art a good sword! On, Ulster and Connaught! Ireland forever! Hew them down, ye men of the fens! We have a doughty captain!"

Even in that boast it was shown that some of Richard's men—not those of Longwood—had doubted him on account of his youth, in spite of the tale of his victory over Clod the Club.

The rush of the French boarders was checked, but not repelled, so many they were and so desperate; but they met now another force. A cunning man was Ben o' Coventry, and fit to be a captain; for he had drawn away a number of Welsh and Irish and some bowmen, for whom there was no room in the waist of the ship. He led them to the prow, which was almost bare of men, save a few archers. It had swung away at first, but now it was hugging closely the high forecastle of La Belle Calaise.

"Forward, my men!" he shouted. "It is our turn to board! Slay as ye go!"

They rushed against a cluster of mere sailor-men, half armed, who had been posted there to keep them out of the way. They were hardly soldiers, although they were fierce enough; and they were mere cattle before the rush of Ben o' Coventry and his mighty followers. The Welshmen spared none of them; and soon the French in the deep waist of La Belle Calaise, pressing forward to reinforce their half-defeated boarders, were suddenly startled by a deadly shower of darts and arrows that fell upon them from their own forecastle. Then, as they turned in dismay, they shouted to their comrades upon the Golden Horn:

"Back! back! lest our own ship be lost. The English have boarded us!"

There was a moment of hesitation; and so at that critical moment no help came to the remaining Frenchmen in the waist of the Golden Horn. They were even outnumbered, since all the archers in the wooden forts fore and aft, twanging their deadly bows almost in safety, counted against the bewildered boarders. No more knights came down from La Belle Calaise. The common men were falling like corn before the reaper.

"On!" shouted Richard. "It is our fight now! Short work is good work!"

The O'Rourke yelled something in the old Erse tongue, and his giants followed him as he fought his way to the side of Richard Neville; but David Griffith summoned his remaining Welshmen, and was followed also by two score of Kentish bowmen, as he hastened forward to join Ben o' Coventry and his daring fellows on the forecastle of La Belle Calaise. It was time, for there were good French knights yet left to lead in a desperate attempt to dislodge them. It was, however, as if the deck or roof of that wooden fort, made with bulwarks and barricades to protect it against all enemies of France, had been just as well prepared to be held by an English garrison. Moreover, all manner of weapons had been put there, ready for use; and among these were pikes and lances with which the Welshmen could thrust at the men who tried to climb the ladders from the waist, while the archers shot for dear life, unerringly.

"My Lord Beaumont," shouted one of the French men-at-arms, "all of our boarders on the English ship are down or taken. Not one is left. Here come the Neville and his tigers. God and St. Denis! We are lost!"

"Courage!" returned Beaumont. "Fight on; we shall overcome them yet!"

But a heavy mace, hurled by a big Cornishman on the forecastle, at that moment smote him on the helm. He fell stunned, while his dismayed comrades shrank back from the storm of English arrows and from the mad rush of Richard and his men-at-arms and the O'Rourke and his Irish axemen.

The French were actually beaten in detail, their greater numbers at no time doing them any good.

In each part of the fight they had had fewer men at the front, and the few that now remained fit to fight seemed to be in a manner surrounded.

"Quarter, if thou wilt surrender!" cried Richard to a knight with closed visor, with whom he was crossing swords.

"Quarter!" came faintly back. "Surrender!" and then he sank upon one knee, for he was wounded by an arrow in the thigh.

"All good knights yield themselves to me!" again shouted Richard in French. "They who hold out are lost!"

More than one of them still fought on in a kind of despair, but others laid down their swords at the feet of Richard. As for any other of the defenders of La Belle Calaise, it was sad to seek them; for the Golden Horn had no man left on board of her save Jack of London at the helm, and the English pikes were everywhere plying mercilessly.

"Leave not one!" shouted the O'Rourke hoarsely to his kerns. "Not one of us had they spared if we had been taken. Let Lord Wartmont care for his gentlemen. They will all pay ransom."

So quickly all was over; and all that was left of the force which that morning had crowded the deck under the brave Monsieur de Gaines was less than half of his brave gentlemen, hardly one of them without a wound.

The Sieur de Beaumont had now recovered his senses ; but as he arose and looked around him, he exclaimed :

"Lord Richard of Wartmont, I would thou wouldst show me the mercy to throw me into the sea. How shall I face my king after such a disgrace as this!"

" 'Twas not thy fault, brave sir," said Richard courteously. "It is the fortune of war. Say to thy king from me, that thy ship was lost when the Comte de Gaines tumbled so many of his force into the Golden Horn. Thou mayest say that he knew not how ready were we to meet him."

"The traitorous Fleming——" began the count, but Richard interrupted him.

"Not traitor to thee," he said. "He is dead indeed ; and his trap caught not us, but thee and thy commander. How art thou now, Sieur de Renly ? I thank thee for slipping well, else thy good sword had done thee better service."

Like a true gentleman, the brave youth spoke kindly to them all, and their hurts were cared for. The several ransoms for each knight were agreed upon ; but they had now no further need for armor, and they were soon appareled only in clothing of wool and linen, or silk and leather, as the case might be.

10

As for the ships, they had sustained small in-
jury in the fight. Now that it was over, the grap-
plings were cast off, and each rode the waves on
its own account. It was hard to provide skilled
crews for both, but a shift was made by dividing
the seamen, and by such selections as could be had
from among the soldiery. Jack of London was
made the sailing master of the Golden Horn, and a
seafaring man from Hull was in like manner put
in charge of La Belle Calaise.

There was now no crowding of men upon either
ship; but there was much care to be given to so
many scores of wounded.

The fog had cleared away, and the Golden
Horn, with her prize, could make a pretty straight
course for La Hogue, thanks to a change in the
wind.

"Art thou hurt at all?" asked Guy the Bow,
when he next met his young commander.

"Nay," said Richard, "unless bruises and
a sore head may count for hurts. But we have
lost a third part of our force, killed or
wounded."

"Well that we lost not all, and our own lives,"
said Guy. "'Twas close work for a while. Glad
am I that our Lady of Wartmont is to hear no bad
news."

"Aye," said Richard; "and now I will tell thee,
thou true man, when I write to her I will bear

thee witness that to thee and Ben o' Coventry is it due that she hath not lost her son."

"I would like her to think well of me," said Guy, smiling with pleasure; "but I pray thee speak well to the prince of the O'Rourke and his long-legged kerns, and of David Griffith. They deserve well of the king."

"Trust me for that," said Richard. "And now, ere the dark hour, I must read my mother's letter. Truth to tell, I could not so much as look at it while I was watching that traitor Fleming, and preparing for what I thought might come. I have already thanked all the men and visited my prisoners. Brave ransom will some of them pay."

"And the prize money for us all," added Guy, with a chuckle. "We may be rich when we return from France."

So he went forward, and Richard sat down to his letter, to read the good words his mother sent him, and to dream of Wartmont and of Longwood, and of the old days before the war.

Then there was sleeping, save for those who could not sleep for their hurts or their misfortunes. It was well on in the forenoon of the following day before the Golden Horn and her captive companion sailed gayly in among the forest of masts that had gathered at La Hogue.

Only a short hour later the young Lord of

Wartmont, with some of his chosen followers and those of his prisoners that were highest in rank, stood in an open space among the camps of King Edward's army.

The king himself was there, and with him were earls and knights and captains not a few. By his side stood the brave Black Prince; but it was to the king that Richard and those who were with him bent the knee, while the young man made his report of the taking of La Belle Calaise.

He was modest enough; but the bright eyes of the prince kindled finely as he heard it, and he said in a low voice to his father:

"Did I not tell thee I was right to intrust a ship to him?"

"The boy did well," said the king dryly, for he was a man hard to please. "Thou Richard of Wartmont, honor to thee and thy merry men all! Thou and the prince are to win spurs of knighthood, side by side, ere we sail again for England. Sir Geoffrey of Harcourt will bid thee where to go."

Richard bent low, and rose to his feet. Sir Geoffrey stepped forward to speak to the Sieur de Renly and the other captured knights. The archers and men-at-arms of Richard's command stood still where they were, waiting for orders; but the Black Prince beckoned Richard aside to get from

him the full particulars of a fray so gallantly
fought and won.

"I envy thee," he said, "thy hand-to-hand
close with De Renly. Thou hast fine war fortune
with thee; and the king is ever better pleased
than he will tell."

It must have been so, for at that moment King
Edward was turning to a noble-looking knight
who stood near him:

"Cousin John Beauchamp of Warwick," he
said, "thou mayest be proud of thy young kinsman. Those of thy blood are apt to make good
captains."

"Thanks, sire," responded the Earl of Warwick,
flushing with pride. "I trust there may never fail
thee plenty of stout Beauchamps and Nevilles to
stand in the front rank of the gallant men of England. But I pray thee, mark how the boy handled
his archers and his Irishmen——"

"And how he watched the traitors and trapped
the treason," laughed a gray-bearded warrior at his
side. "He hath his wits about him."

"Yea, Norfolk," said the king with a gloom
upon his face; "the men who are to defend England and defeat her enemies must watch against
treason by night and by day. 'Twas a Fleming that set the trap for the Golden Horn; and
the men who are to march with us against
Philip of Valois are all from our own islands.

Not a man below a man-at-arms can even speak French."

So the king's wisdom spoke for itself, while Sir Geoffrey of Harcourt and the prince sent Richard Neville and his brave men to the camp where they were to pass the night; for the whole army was to march away next morning.

CHAPTER VII.

THE exact place of the landing of King Edward had been at a harbor called St. Vast, northerly from Cape La Hogue, and the King of France believed him still at sea, on his way to Gascony or Guienne, that there he might strike a blow for the sadly beset forces of the Earl of Derby. There was no need for camping long on the shore that the English forces might be put into good marching order. Even as they landed their proper divisions were assigned them. When the next morning sun arose, it was known to all that the king had named the Earl of Arundel his constable, to abide with himself; also that he had named the Earl of Warwick and Sir Geoffrey of Harcourt marshals of the army. The left wing was to be commanded on the march by Sir Geoffrey, and the right wing by the earl. All who were to be with the earl, however, were moving along the coast, southerly, in the morn. In like manner went the fleet, taking many prizes of armed ships and merchantmen.

It was the earl's first errand to take or to dis-
able a place called Barfleur, where was a very strong
castle, that from it might come forth no harm to
any English force to be left at the St. Vast landing.

Side by side rode Richard and his uncle, and
the earl questioned him much of his doings on the
Golden Horn.

"Thou hast done well," he said, "but I like it
not that thou art with me. It were better thou
shouldst ride with Harcourt. Seest thou not that,
as we are ordered now, he will lead the van and I
the rear guard? I shall take these towns and many
another, but he will be first at Caen, and that is the
prize of Normandy."

"I hear 'tis a great place," said Richard, "but
I like it that to us it is given to strike the first
blow in France."

Even as he spoke a mounted scout came galloping back to report that Barfleur was in sight,
and that English war ships were sailing into the
harbor.

The earl drew rein and raised his baton, utter-
ing no word; but a hundred or so of men-at-arms
who were behind him shouted loudly and dashed
by, spurring toward the front.

"Thy bowmen next!" shouted the earl to Richard. "Follow the knights closely. The pikemen
are already far ahead. If it be God's will, we will
sweep the town in an hour."

Hotly rushed Richard's blood as he pressed on, followed by three hundred of the archers of Arden. Hardly he knew what time had passed after that until he found himself halted to watch while axe-men battered at a town gate and pikemen placed ladders to mount a wall. His archers meantime were making targets of whoever might show himself among the wall battlements.

"Is this the way a town is taken?" he exclaimed. "I deemed there were more delay. There go the good knights, up the ladders and through the gate! 'Twas but badly made, to be broken in so soon. On, men of Arden! Follow me!"

Follow they did, and some good archery work befell them after they entered the town, but the English were even too many for the capture and pillage of so small a place.

"It was no battle, my Lord," Richard said to the earl two hours later, as they met in the great square in the center of the town. "But we have taken Barfleur."

"That have we," said the earl, "and that is all. Look yonder!"

Across long rows of intervening houses gazed the young captain as the earl pointed. There was a rocky height, and upon it arose the towers and the turreted walls of a great castle.

"I see," said Richard. "It hath a strong look. How shall we take it?"

"Not at all," replied the earl marshal, laughing. "He who holdeth it for the King of France refused to yield it, and well he may. We could hammer at it in vain all summer. All the need is to hem in the garrison somewhat by the taking of the town. The English army will march on and waste no time. Take thou therefore a lesson in good war craft. Thy king will make no blunder of throwing away strength upon mere stone work on a hill calling itself a castle."

"I will bear it in mind," said Richard. "I would have thought it must needs be taken."

Loud laughed the earl marshal, but already his officers were recalling the troops from the sacking of the town, that all his force might turn again to rejoin the army of the king, that had been marching northward.

Stretched out along the roads and levels, but moving steadily, were all the divisions of the forces of King Edward. The last of them, with much munition of war, was even now disembarking from the shipping at St. Vast, for it taketh care and time to transfer horses and matters of weight from a deck to a beach. When the night fell all camps were made with care, as became good generalship, although there was fair certainty that no considerable armed force of foemen could be near at hand.

Morn came, and in its first hours Richard was galloping on to the center with a writing from the

Earl of Warwick to the king, but to the prince was it delivered, and he read.

"This to my father," said he heartily ; "but I am glad that the earl should please to have thee with me and with Harcourt. And thou hast seen a town taken? Never the same saw I, and I know not how I am to win spurs tramping these roads without a French man-at-arms in sight !"

Nevertheless he went to the king and came again, and they twain rode on together talking of the war.

"The earl sendeth word," said the prince, "that he will waste no time nor men in vainly besieging the castle of Cherbourg. We need it not, but we shall sack Carenton before to-morrow night."

"Knoweth the king," asked Richard, "at what place mustereth the host of France?"

"Our last news," replied the prince, "putteth Philip in Aquitaine, full far away from Paris. Were the king so minded he could get there first."

"And take the capital city of France?" exclaimed Richard. "That were grand! We shall press onward, then?"

"That will we," said the prince, "but not to take a city we can not hold. Small good were it to be shut up there by half the hosts of Europe. But we can draw away the French from Derby's front, and we can win Calais."

"Win Calais by a march through Normandy?"
sprang from the lips of Richard. "I see not well
how that can be. What were Calais, compared
with Paris?"

"It is the sorest thorn in the side of England,
saith my father," replied the prince. "Even the
Channel and the British seas are but half our own
while that harbor is a refuge for the fleets of
France and a nesting place for all manner of
pirates. We must take and hold it, as we hold
Dover. It hath but one strong defense."

"I have heard that its walls are strong," said
Richard, "and that it can stand a long siege by
sea and land."

"Long and hard it well may be," laughed the
prince, "but sieges have an end, and towns are taken
if the besiegers themselves be not routed in their
camps. The defense of Calais against us is this
army of the King of France. Until that shall be
utterly beaten the town is safe. Thou wilt yet
see clearly the wisdom of the king."

There was another night's camping and the
Carenton town surrendered, but the castle thereof
detained Earl Warwick and his power during
two more days, while the main host marched on.
Town after town that lay along its broad road of
desolation either opened its gates without resistance or was shortly stormed and plundered. Long
lines of wains were all the while traveling back to St.

Vast and other seaports, that the ships might convey the captured goods and treasures to safe keeping in England.

This was the manner of all warring in those
days, and sore was the distress of the people of
Normandy. They were brave enough, but they
had neither great captains nor any central body of
an army whereunto they might rally. For their
mere numbers they could have eaten up the English army, but what are numbers that are scattered
vainly over a great province?

Daily did the prince and Richard draw nearer
to each other, as they found occasion for meeting; but the duties of the young heir of Wartmont were now with the advance, under Sir
Geoffrey of Harcourt. Small fighting had he
seen, but many a deed of pillage that was sad to
look upon, and he was learning how terrible a
thing is war.

"God keep it from merry England!" he often
thought, and yet he knew that all the messengers
from home brought rumors that a Scottish host
was gathering fast to take advantage of King Edward's absence.

"Evil to them!" he said angrily. "If the good
archbishop be also training the men of the north
counties and the middle, I trust Sir Robert Johnstone will face them with bowmen as good as
are those of Longwood and Arden. We can

give him no aid, but to-morrow we shall get to Caen."

The prince was with the king that night and Richard saw him not. Nor was there message for him to carry in the morn, but there came to him a summons from Marshal de Harcourt.

"Richard of Wartmont," said his captain when they met, "Sir Thomas Holland and Sir Peter Legh, with knights and men-at-arms, form the advance on Caen. With them go thou and double thy number of the archers of Arden. With thee will also be the Irish and the Welsh, for I learn that the people of this town have gone mad with conceit. They will face us outside of their walls. If we may break their front, we may enter Caen in their foolish company."

Like word went back to the king, praying him to hasten, that he might see his standard lifted over the capital of Normandy.

Good was the planning of De Harcourt, for, as the English van emerged early that day, behold a numerous but motley and ill-ordered array of armed citizens and country folk, drawn out to meet them. With them were many knights and men-at-arms, but the marshal spoke truly when he said of them:

"An army that is not an army. We will scatter them like chaff!"

"Seest thou yonder town?" asked Sir Thomas

Holland of Richard, as they paused on the brow of a low hill to let the bowmen come up.

Richard looked earnestly, for the walls were wide-reaching, and they seemed to be high and strong. On one side of the great town arose a castle of surpassing splendor, and he had heard that the Governor of Caen, Sir John de Blargny, held it with three hundred Genoese crossbowmen and other forces. There were church spires also, and of these arose one higher than the rest, at which Sir Thomas pointed with his lance.

" In a crypt of that church," he said, " rest the bones of William the Conqueror. From this town did he and his host march to the overthrow of King Harold at Hastings."

Richard gazed in silence, but he heard strange words among the bowmen behind him, speaking the ancient tongue.

" 'Tis good hearing," said Guy the Bow. " As he and his Normans did to England, so have the Saxons under King Edward done to Normandy. The conquest is ours this time ! "

" The tables are turned," said Ben of Coventry, " and rare hath been the plundering. But we have yet fought no fight like that of Hastings. Until then we shall not be even with the French. I shall shoot closely that day when it shall come."

Deep, therefore, was the bitterness that grew from the old time. Alas, that it did not cease,

and that during centuries more the old feud
rankled murderously in the hearts of Englishmen,
so that even their Norman kings made use of it
as a power whereby to rally armies to fight the
outland men beyond the sea!

Forward now dashed the English van, all
shouting loudly, but no battle did await them.
Mayhap they were in greater force than the men
of Caen expected, or that the latter bethought
them suddenly how good were stone walls to fight
behind. At all events, there were few volleys of
arrows sent before the French muster broke and
ran back in confusion toward the open gates.

"Forward!" shouted Sir Thomas. "The middle gateway! There be good knights there, all
tangled in the press. They can neither fight nor
flee. Brave ransom to be won! Press on!"

Even he and his own knights could make little
better speed than might the bowmen on foot, but
the French men-at-arms were already jammed one
against another in the narrow passage by which
they had hoped to retreat into the city. There
could be no closing of the gate, but over it was a
small fortalice, with a broad stairway leading up
to it. Down sprang the good knights, for here
seemed a refuge, as if it were a place wherein they
might defend themselves.

Much rather was it a trap in which they were
to be taken helplessly. In vain they manned the

battlements, for up the stairway after them poured Richard Neville's bowmen and axemen, with Sir Thomas Holland, Sir Peter Legh, and a dozen other knights.

"Down with them, Richard of Wartmont!" shouted Guy the Bow, and the shafts began to fly.

But in front of the Frenchmen in that tower stepped forth a knight in gorgeous armor, who shouted boldly:

"Sir Thomas Holland, dost thou not know thine old-time comrade against the Prussian heathen and the Saracens of Grenada? I am the Count of Eu and Guignes, Constable of France, and with me is the Count of Tancarville. These all be knights of note. But we are betrayed to thine hand by these cowardly townspeople."

So they surrendered all, while through the gateway below dashed Sir Geoffrey of Harcourt, his men-at-arms, and a great tide of spearmen and bowmen. At no great distance behind them rode the king and the prince, and it was but little before the Earl of Northampton raised the royal standard over that very gateway fort in token that Caen had fallen.

The walls were won, indeed, but not the whole town or the castle. On to the center and to the townhall pressed Harcourt, and with him now was Richard. Every house was a small fort, however, and all doors were closed and barred. Not for

11

their goods only, but for their very lives, did the inhabitants of Caen believe themselves to be contending. In the upper stories and garrets of the buildings had they prepared munitions of heavy stones, beams, and the like, and these did they now rain down upon the ranks of the English soldiery. Many were slain or wounded thereby. Brave knights were stricken from their horses to lie helpless upon the pavement.

All these things were witnessed by the king himself when he and the prince and those who were with them rode through the gate of the city. An angry man was he to be stoned and to narrowly escape destruction in a street of a place which he had already taken.

Sir Geoffrey and his men were at the town-hall now, and one of their first works had been to search for and to seize the official records and archives. It had been better for Normandy if all these things had perished, but none had looked for so sudden an entry of the English, so that the writings remained. These were delivered to the king on his arrival. He read from page to page, and his hot wrath burned yet more hotly. Among the captured manuscripts was one under the seal royal of France, and it was a covenant between the King and the people of Caen and of Normandy for their service against the English king. Already had there been good proof that the Normans had

greatly favored an invasion of England like that
of William the Conqueror. Here was fresh proof
thereof, with more that was as poison.

Fierce and hasty was the next speech of the
angry king, for he commanded that the city should
be given up to sack and pillage, without mercy
to man or woman. It had been a terrible deed to
do, for the soldiery were greatly enraged already,
and some of their deeds had been cruel. Well
was it then for all that Sir Geoffrey of Harcourt
was a wise man and humane as well as a good war
captain, for he spoke plainly to King Edward.

"Dear sire," he said, "restrain thy courage a
little, I pray thee, and be satisfied with what
thou hast done. Thou hast a long journey before thou shalt get to Calais, where thou intendest
to go."

Much more he said and argued, and all the
while the king grew calmer.

"Sir Geoffrey," he replied at last, "thou art
our marshal; therefore order as thou shalt please,
for this time we wish not to interfere."

Nevertheless, in the speech of the marshal had
been published the secret counsel of the king and
the real purpose of the campaign from before the
army left England. There were those even in
later days who maintained that Edward had sailed
at a venture, and had marched at random, without
set plan or purpose, but they knew him not very

well, nor did they hear his chief captain answer him at Caen thus early in the campaign.

Out rode then Sir Geoffrey from street to street, with banners displayed, declaring full mercy to the townsfolk if they would cease fighting, and commanding, on pain of death, that no English soldier should harm or insult either man or woman.

So the massacre was stayed, but for all that there was vast plunder taken.

Richard was with the prince once more for a little while, and to him he spoke of the purpose of the Normans to invade England.

"They thought to do as in Harold's time," he said. "There had been great mischief, truly, if they could have landed."

"Not so," replied the prince. "I heard Sir Geoffrey and the king on that head. No other battle of Hastings could have come, for the Archbishop of York hath force enough to face the Scots. King Harold had to fight and beat the Welsh first, and then the Northmen under Hardrada, before he turned, with what army he had left, to meet William of Normandy. An invasion now would meet the whole array of England at one field, with Welsh and Irish many thousands. Moreover, in England there were neither forts nor castles in Harold's day, while now there are too many for the peace of the realm. So said my royal father, for the castles can be well held even against the power of the king."

"The Saxons fought well," said Richard.

"Aye, that did they," replied the prince, "and well do we know that thou and thine are of them. Wilt thou tell me, Richard of Wartmont, why thou and thy Saxons all are so strong for the Crown? Are we not of Norman blood?"

"Yea, that ye are," said Richard, "but of Saxon royalty of descent as well. We all do know that truth. But above all do the people of every kindred look to see the king stand between them and the barons. So are we his lithsmen, nor can any take us out of his hand. He is our king!"

"Stay where thou art!" exclaimed the prince; "I will bear that word to the king ere it is cold in my thought."

Away he rode, and he had to dismount and enter the townhall before he could have speech with his father. That which he said was heard by no other ears, but the face of the king grew red with pleasure.

"Truly," he said low-voiced, "the youth and his people are wiser than I knew! Herein is a point of statecraft fit to be an heirloom of the British kings. I will wear it. The king of the people hath no need to fear the power of his barons. I have seen it long. There shall be more and larger parliaments henceforth, and the

Commons may speak their will freely. I am less at the bidding of my proud earls. I have henceforth no fear of Philip of France, but I must win Calais, if only for the good of my merchant-men. We will march thither speedily, as soon as I shall have smitten hard this huge mustering of Philip the unwise."

The prince came not back, nor did he afterward give to Richard the words of the king; but the writers who in due season recorded the history of those times had many things to write concerning the kindly relations that grew up between Edward and the Commons, especially all merchants and artisans and seafaring men.

There were days of seeming rest for the army, but these were largely spent in good training, lest discipline should have been injured on the march. On one of these days came a summons from Sir Geoffrey of Harcourt to Richard Neville, and when he obeyed it he found the two marshals together. Earl Warwick was the first to speak.

"Good news for thee, Richard," he said. "Thy gateway fort was a fine trap for thy fortune. The king hath purchased of Sir Thomas Holland, Sir Peter Legh, and the knights and thee, the ransom of the Constable of France and Lord Tancarville. He payeth twenty thousand rose nobles of gold, and thy share will be made good. All thy other prizes will be sure to thee in my

own hand, for I send all to thy mother at Warwick. Thou wilt be richer than was ever thy
father, if thou shalt hold on as thou hast begun."

Great was the joy of Richard, and earnest were
his thanks to the kindly earl; but he had now to
hear from his commander.

"Hearken thou well," he said. "Take thou
thine own companies and such as shall be named
to thee by Sir Peter Legh. March out at the
northern gate and follow the road he will name to
thee. Speak not to any concerning thy errand,
and thou thyself hast need to know no more. But
if any stranger shall attempt to march with thee,
slay thou him on the spot."

"See that thou obey in silence," added the earl.
"I trust in God that I shall see thee again, but
do thou thy duty utterly caring not for thy blood
or thy life."

Richard bowed low, for his heart was dancing
within him at the prospect of new adventure, and
he did but say:

"God save the king! And I pray thee, tell
my mother I did my duty utterly."

"Go thou," said the earl.

"Haste thee also," came from Sir Geoffrey,
"for thine is the vanguard."

O what pride for one so young—to be ordered to the front of a secret foray!

Nevertheless, in the very street, as Richard rode

to the camp of his bowmen, he was met and halted by the prince.

"Richard of Wartmont," he said, but not loud-ly, "thou hast thy orders?"

Richard bowed low.

"So have I mine!" exclaimed the prince. "Not all the fortune of this campaign is to be thine alone. Thou shalt see me with my sword out before thou art older. There are blows to strike, and I am to be in the *mêlée*, as becomes me. Haste thee now, and fare thee well until I see thee again."

It had been ill to answer in words, but Richard bowed again and rode onward.

It was at the gate that he met Sir Peter Legh with further instructions. A good knight was Sir Peter and broad in the shoulders, but he stood a fathom and half a handbreadth in his stature—a sore antagonist for any man to face in field or tourney, and having experience of many a hard-fought field.

"Thou of Wartmont," he said dryly, "since I am to have company of thee and thine, well. It is De Harcourt's word to me. He is my com-mander. Thou mayest lead older and better men fairly enough. I will tell thee what to do."

"I was ahead of all but thee in the gate of Caen," responded Richard a little freely, for he was but young in temper. "Thou wilt not find me a pace behind thee if so be there is fighting or climbing to be done."

"That there will be," growled Sir Peter. "Thou art nimble enough, but other men are bigger in the bones. But it is said of thee that thou hast good fortune, and that is a grand thing in a fray. I will go to thy men with thee and learn what timber I am to build with."

So strong in the minds of all men was the belief that even more than lance or sword or counsel was the thing they called fortune. But better for the army and for the taking of Calais were the long preparation and the subtle wisdom of Edward the Third.

Few were the words of Sir Peter as they twain rode onward, save to give his youthful comrade full and clear directions as to the road by which he was to march. He knew, however, that the burly knight eyed him keenly from time to time, as if he were trying to read what value he might have as a soldier.

Then came they to the camp, and Sir Peter turned his eyes in like manner upon Guy the Bow and the men of Longwood.

"I ask the marshal's pardon," he grumbled testily. "If their chief be only a boy, his clansmen are long in the legs. Every man a pardoned outlaw, I am told, and half of kin to the Neville. Look you!" he spoke loudly to Guy the Bow, "ye all are to march with Richard of Wart-mont."

"Aye, Sir Peter," said Guy. "He is our captain. We have fought for him ere this, shoulder to shoulder."

"Thou art malapert!" exclaimed Sir Peter. "Guard thou thy tongue, lest I teach thee a lesson thou needest. The lash is near thee!"

Hot as fire glowed the brown cheeks of Guy the Bow, and he strode one pace nearer.

"I know thee, Sir Peter Legh," he said. "Thou art a good lance enough, but who gave thee the ill wisdom to speak of the lash to the free archers of Arden?"

Right well astonished was Sir Peter, for at every side, as he looked beyond Guy, did the tall foresters spring to their feet, and full a score of them had arrows on the string. He heard rough speaking in a tongue which he did not fully understand, but one voice that was louder than the rest was of ordinary English.

"We are not dogs, nor serfs, nor villains," it declared, "that we should be whipped for free speech. We are free men. If yonder man-at-arms layeth but a finger upon Guy the Bow or upon my Lord of Wartmont, I will send this shaft through his midriff."

"Richard Neville, what meaneth this?" exclaimed Sir Peter Legh. "Whose men are these?"

"We belong to the Wartmont, under the Earl of Warwick," spoke out Ben of Coventry, "and through the earl we are the king's men. Look thou well to that."

"Sir Peter," said Richard sturdily, "there was no cause of offense to thee."

"These, then, are yeomen?" asked Sir Peter, with a grim smile that meant much.

"Never was collar of serf upon the neck of an archer of Arden," replied Richard. "Free they were born, and free they will die. And I swear to thee that my father's son will die here with them ere they are harmed."

The knight was wiser than he had seemed, for he did but laugh loudly.

"I have no quarrel to pick with Earl Warwick or with thee, or with thy deerstealers," he said. "Bring them along. These were with thee when thou didst take La Belle Calaise? Pirates every man. But they are what thou wilt need to have with thee if thou art to follow Sir Thomas Holland and me. The old one-eyed Saracen fighter will lead where none but brave hearts may go."

All the men heard him, and bows were promptly lowered. Said Guy the Bow:

"My speech was not malapert for such as I am, Sir Knight. Thou didst ill to threaten free-men. But it may be, if thou art in a press, thou wilt be pleased to hear at thy side the twang-

ing of the good bows of Longwood and Wartmont."

"That will I, merry men all," said Sir Peter
heartily. "Well do I know now why ye were
chosen by Harcourt. Ye are of the old midland
breed of wolves that die silent but biting. 'Tis
your proverb."

More did he say as he walked among them;
but he inspected their weapons, as became a captain, and there came also pack beasts laden with
sheaves of arrows, that every quiver might be full.

"Richard of Wartmont," he said at parting,
"there is naught but good will between me and
thee. English am I, and greatly do I like thy men.
We were but a lost people if our yeomanry
were no higher spirited than are the slavish rabble
that will swarm behind the nobles of France and
their unwise, cunning king. As for him, he will
find that the double tongue fitted to cheat by an
embassage is of small value in the right handling
of an army. He may learn something yet from
our Edward of England. Unless Geoffrey of Harcourt is a false witness, and unless the king's plan
goeth too far astray, Calais will ere long be but
an English port. Meet thou me as I bade thee,
for I must go."

Even so he did, but Richard remained to com-
plete the right ordering of his command. Anxious
indeed was he, and he brought to mind every les-

son of war that he had learned in England or on
the march. Who could tell, he thought darkly,
what desperate venture might be at hand? Careless captains do but throw away what heedful men
might win. Above all was it heavy upon his mind
that on this occasion he and his had been chosen to
guard the prince himself, as being such as the king
could rely upon to the very death.

"So, if he dieth," said he, "I and mine will not
return to face the king. Where lieth his body,
there will mine be found, and all the men of Arden
and Longwood with me."

Also in like manner responded the archers
themselves when he arrayed them and told them,
passing the word from man to man:

"We are the Black Prince's comrades, this day
and night. It is the king's trust."

"We will keep trust," they said.

CHAPTER VIII.

SPLENDID to look upon was the advance of King Edward's army from Caen, with its banners, its mailclad horsemen, its winding rivers of shields, and the flashing of the sunlight on the helmets and on the points of polished steel.

The roads were dusty, but their dryness gave good footing, and all wagon wheels rolled well. There was a hindrance in the narrowness of all the Normandy highways and byways, for it compelled Edward to divide his forces and send them forward by several lines of march. His being there could now be known to Philip of France at once, but the great French army was still in Gascony, beleaguering the stout Earl of Derby and his forces. There was therefore no power to block the progress of the English invaders, although each of their divisions had somewhat to contend with. There were walled towns and there were fortresses. In some of these were not only garrisons, but much plunder, and their taking would be required by the military plans of the king. His generalship was greatly exhibited in this, that by landing so unexpectedly in Normandy, and by then marching straight across country, as if his aim were to take Paris, he compelled Philip to loosen his grip upon the army of the Earl of Derby, and to march his mighty host with all speed to the saving of his own capital.

Town after town had surrendered to Edward, and many castles had opened their gates without a fight, yet not all. The country people had suffered sorely, for the army required much in the way of provisions, but the scourge of war fell most heavily upon the rich, and on such as made resistance.

Richard Neville was now honored with the command of a goodly detachment. With him, as before on the Golden Horn, were men-at-arms and footmen of every kind, for so had the king ordered for all parts of his advance.

The heir of Wartmont was this day so far separated from the main body of the king's army that it was almost as if he were invading that part of Normandy by himself, in command of a small army of his own.

"My Lord," said a man-at-arms who rode at his side, "if thou wilt permit the question, art thou sure of thy direction? Were we to stray too far, we might meet with reproof, or worse."

"This is the road that Sir Geoffrey Harcourt bade me take," replied Richard. "But I would we had a guide."

They were well in advance of their little column, and they rode out over the brow of a low hill and from under the shadow of overarching trees.

"My Lord of Wartmont," loudly exclaimed the man-at-arms, "look yonder! Shall we not push forward?"

Before them lay a deep, narrow valley, with many cots and vineyards scattered up and down the stream which wandered through it. Directly across the hollow, however, there was a sight worth seeing. High and rock-bordered was that northward hillside, but on its crown was a fortress that was half a church, with a walled town beyond the foot of the castle. High and precipitous were the granite cliffs, high were the towers of the castle, but into the sunset light above them all arose the cross-tipped steeple of the church.

On this side of the outer wall of the town on the hill was a great gate, and over it floated, as also on the donjon keep of the castle, near the town gate, the golden lilies of the royal standard of France, streaming out against the sky.

"We will not go forward," said Richard. "We will halt, rather. No force like ours can do aught

with a fort like that. Nor shall we now surprise
them. Some captain of high rank is in command,
for there is the *fleur-de-lis* flag."

"My Lord, there was the blast of a horn!" said
Ben o' Coventry, from the archer ranks.

"Thou hast keen hearing," Richard replied, as
again the mellow music came faintly up the road;
"that horn calleth us to wait for the force that fol-
loweth."

At the word of command, the horsemen drew
rein and the footmen stood at rest. They had not
long to wait.

A splendid black horse, and on him a rider in
black armor, came spurring along the narrow highway accompanied only by a page.

"It is the prince!" exclaimed Richard. "What
doeth he here alone?"

So loudly was it spoken, and so near was the
young royal hero of England, that the answer came
from his own lips.

"Not alone am I, Richard Neville, but I have
outridden Wakeham to speed on and warn thee not
to show thyself beyond the ridge, lest thou warn
the warders of Bruyerre that we are at hand.
Halt, thou and thine!"

"My Lord Prince Edward, we are halted, with
that very thought in mind," respectfully answered
Richard. "But is yonder place Bruyerre?"

"It is, indeed," said the prince. "'Tis a strong-
12

hold since the days of Norman Rollo. Duke Robert also was besieged there once."

"How, then, shall we take it?" came regretfully
from Richard's lips. "It were not well to leave it
untaken."

"That will we not," said the Prince, "and glad
am I have to thee with me. For that end we sent
thee ahead. Sir Henry and I had few enough
of men, and they are mostly men-at-arms. We
need thy Irish kerns,* and thy Welsh, and thy
bowmen."

"Here they come, my Lord!" Guy the Bow
announced from among the archers. "They all
are riding hard as if for a charge."

A brave array of knights and gentlemen in full
armor came fast through the dust clouds of their
own raising. Beside the foremost horseman rode
one who carried no arms at all. On his head was
the plain cap of a tradesman, and from under it
long white hair came down to his shoulders. He
rode firmly despite his years, however, and there
was a kind of eager light upon his deeply wrinkled
face.

"All is well!" he exclaimed. "My Lord of
Wakeham, the prince reached them in time, and
they are halted."

"Aye, and I would there were more of them,"

* The kern was a light-armed foot soldier, who usually carried a
spear and knife.

replied Sir Henry. "Our own footmen are long miles behind, and the day is waning."

"We need night, not day, for the taking of Bruyerre," said the old man gloomily. "Even now we were wise to get into some safe hiding. There is a forest glen to the right of where the prince is waiting."

In a few minutes more Sir Henry rode to the side of the prince and held out a hand to Richard.

"Thy men are in good condition," he said; "and that is as it should be, for they have sharp work before them."

"Ready are we," said Richard, but his eyes were upon the face of the white-haired man.

He sat in silence, gazing across the valley at the towers and walls of the fortress, and he seemed moved by strong emotions.

"What sayest thou, Giles Monson ?" asked the prince. "Are there changes ?"

"In me, my Prince," responded Giles, "but not in yonder town. A Christian man am I this day, and it is not given me to judge, but I am a true Englishman. With an honest heart and in good faith did I bring steel wares from Sheffield to the wicked Lord of Bruyerre. False and cruel was he, a robber and a villain. He laughed at me when once I was in his power. Fourteen years was I a prisoner in yonder keep, and I grew old before my time.

Behold the scars of fetters on my wrists. Then was I a beggar and a starveling in the town for three years more, watched always and beaten oft. But I learned every inch of yonder hill, and at last I made my escape. By the path along which I left Bruyerre can I guide this army in. But there must be ladders stronger than the cord I came down upon."

"A dozen are with our own foot soldiers," said Sir Henry. "But haste now, lest we be discovered from the castle."

All riders were dismounting, and Richard went into the woods with his forest men to seek the glen spoken of by Giles. It was not far to find, and it led on down into the valley.

The forest growth was old and dense, and, once the soldiery marched well in, they were completely hidden. Only a strong guard waited at the wayside to intercept all passengers, and here at last came Richard, just as the sun went down.

"The prince's foot soldiers will arrive soon," said the young leader to Guy the Bow. Ben o' Coventry was peering over the ridge of the hill, and he came back hastily.

"Men from the castle, my Captain!" he exclaimed. "A knight, I should say by his crest, and four esquires, with mounted serving men a half dozen. The knight, I noted, rideth with visor up."

"Thinking not of any foe," Richard answered. "We will hide under the trees and let them go by. Then will we close behind them."

"We could smite them as they come," said Guy.

"Nay," replied Richard, "lest even so much as one on horseback escape to warn the town."

Word was sent to the prince, and soon he was there, having posted his troops in the glen, and with him came Sir Henry of Wakeham. It was no moment for speech, for the French cavalcade came gayly over the hill.

Silent and motionless, the English in their ambush almost held their breath until the party from Bruyerre was a bowshot past them. Then out into the road they poured as silently, and the trap was set.

"They will meet our foot right soon," said Sir Henry, "but they will not risk a charge upon five hundred men. They will come back."

"Sir Thomas Gifford will render a good account of them, if they do not," replied the prince.

Not more than half a mile down the road and around a bend of it, at that hour, pressed on the English foot. At their head rode one knight only, with a few men-at-arms, and not far behind him strode a brawny, red-haired man, who shouted back to those behind him, in Irish:

"Forward now, ye men of the fens, of Connaught and of Ulster! Yet a little, and we shall be with our brave boy of the Golden Horn and of La Belle Calaise, and with the prince and Sir Henry."

It was the O'Rourke himself, promoted to a better command, with full leave to arm his giants with axes, in honor of his feats in the sea fight. In like manner the rear guard was led by David Griffith, and the weapons of the Welshmen were such as those with which their ancestors had fought the Roman legions of Cæsar and the Saxons of Harold the King.

"Who cometh?" exclaimed Sir Thomas, for at that moment the party of French from Bruyerre had seen his banner and his ranks, and they had promptly turned round to speed back to the castle.

"The English!" they shouted. "The pirates of Albion! Back to the town!"

They had no dreams of aught but a swift, unhindered escape; and the greater was their astonishment to find their way blocked below the hill ridge by a dense mass of pikemen and bowmen, in front of whom stood a dozen armored knights. There was no use in either flight or fighting; and their leader reversed his lance and rode forward.

"Yield thee!" rang out in English. "I am Sir Henry of Wakeham."

"Needs must!" responded the knight in Norman French. "I am Guilbert, Sieur de Cluse. I had visited with Raoul de Bruyerre, my kinsman, and I was but riding homeward. Alas, the day!"

He and his party dismounted and were disarmed. They were doubly astonished at meeting the prince himself with what seemed so small a force, and the Sieur de Cluse remarked with something of bitterness:

"Little ye know of the nut ye think to crack. De Bruyerre hath gathered three thousand men, and he is provisioned for a siege."

"Not more than that?" exclaimed the prince. "Glad am I of thy news. I had feared he had greater force. We have almost half that number of our own. The castle and the town are ours!"

The prisoners were led under the trees, and now the night came on, and it was fairly sure that there would be no more wayfarers. Little more could be learned, except that all the townspeople were as well armed and ready as the garrison.

Every plan had been well laid beforehand. Only an hour after sunset dense clouds covered the sky, insuring perfect darkness. Out, down the glen, swept David Griffith and his Welshmen, to seize all roads leading to the castle gate. Along the highway itself rode the prince and his mounted force—a hundred and thirty steel-clad horsemen. Behind them marched the greater part of the English foot; but by another path went Sir Henry of

Wakeham, Richard Neville, and Sir Thomas Gifford. With them were the O'Rourke and two
hundred Irish, and two hundred bowmen of Warwick and Kent. The scaling ladders were with
these.

Away to the right, across fields and through
vineyards, Giles Monson led the way. He was
still unarmed, save for a stout "Sheffield whittle,"
a foot long, sheathed, in his belt. Hardly a word
he spoke until his companions found themselves at
the foot of a perpendicular crag.

"There is a break twenty feet up," he said,
"and a flat place. From that point our peril be-
ginneth. Silence, all!"

A ladder was placed, and up he went like a
squirrel. A low whistle was heard as he reached
the top of the ladder; the signal came from Richard,
just behind him. Next came a clang of steel, for
the heir of Wartmont had smitten down a half-
slumbering sentinel.

Up poured the English, headed by Sir Henry;
they brought a second ladder with them and others
were placing it at the foot of the crag.

"A shorter ladder will do for this next mounting," whispered Giles Monson. "Then there is a
wall, but sentries are seldom posted there."

Hardly had he spoken before a voice above
them hailed in French:

"Who cometh there?"

Up went the ladder, and on it the English climbed fast.

A flight of arrows answered him, and no second question came down. Up went the ladder and on it the English climbed fast. The wall, when they reached it, was but a dozen feet high, and was hardly an obstacle. Beyond it Sir Henry halted until many men stood beside him. Then he spoke in a low tone.

"Pass the word," he said. "Pause not for aught, but follow me to the castle and the town gate. We must win that and let in the prince, though all die who are here."

He strode forward then, and ever in front of him went Giles Monson, his cap in his hand and his white hair flying.

Few lights were burning in any of the build-ings, for it was long after curfew. There were no wayfarers along the narrow, winding streets through which, avoiding the middle of the town, Giles Mon-son guided the English. Hardly a weapon clanged, and no word was spoken, for every man knew that if an alarm were given too soon so small a force would be overwhelmed and all must die.

"Yon is the gate," whispered Giles at last. "'Tis a fort of itself, and it needs must have a strong guard."

"They are on the watch for foes from without," said Sir Henry. "Richard Neville, show thyself a good man-at-arms! Charge in at yonder portal with thy Irish, and we will form behind thee and press on to open the town gates and hold them."

The O'Rourke heard the command and he whistled shrilly to his men; still in front of Richard, through the deep gloom, flitted the white-haired guide, for the portal at which Sir Henry pointed; to the left was the open gate of the great tower, the donjon keep, the citadel of Bruyerre. A moat there was, but the bridge was in place, and the guards in armor were lolling lazily.

"Charge! For the king!" shouted Richard, as he sprang swiftly along the bridge; he dashed past the guards and was within the portal before they could draw their swords. Down they went under the Irish axes, and so the entrance to the keep was won. Then the fighting began, for there were many brave men in the citadel of Bruyerre and they were awaking. But they came out of their quarters in sudden bewilderment, singly or in squads, and in the dim light they at first hardly knew friend from foe. Scores were smitten in utter darkness by unseen hands, and everywhere were panic and confusion among the defenders.

"On!" shouted Giles Monson. "My Lord of Wartmont, I lead thee to the chamber of De Bruyerre!"

They were at the head of a flight of stairs, and before them was a long passage lighted by hanging lamps. Into the passage had rushed out—from

the sleeping rooms on either side—a dozen swordsmen, and some of them had bucklers. Well was
it for Richard then that Guy the Bow and the
Longwood foresters had believed it their duty to
follow their own young captain, for otherwise he
had been almost alone. From the archers whizzed
shaft after shaft, and hardly did he cross swords
with any knight before the Frenchman's blade fell
from his hand.

One towering form in a long blue robe was behind the others.

"Who are ye, in Heaven's name?" he had
shouted. "St. Denis, they are fiends!"

"My Lord Raoul de Bruyerre," fiercely responded Giles Monson, "'tis the vengeance of
Heaven upon thy false heart and thy cruelty. I
am thy Sheffield man, thou robber!"

"Yield thee, my Lord of Bruyerre!" shouted
Richard; but along the passage darted Giles Monson, bent on revenge.

"Thou art the traitor!" cried De Bruyerre,
and drawing his sword he sprang to strike down
the advancing Englishman. Too eager to heed
his own safety, Giles Monson leaped upon the
French knight and struck fiercely with his long
dagger.

Both weapons reached their marks.

"Thou villain, thou hast slain the knight!"
cried Richard. "He might have surrendered."

But Giles Monson had fallen beneath the sword
of his victim, and would never speak more.

"Stay not here!" Richard commanded. "Follow me! The keep is not half taken."

It was but the truth, and yet the remaining
fight was only to make all sure. One strong party
of French soldiers was beaten because they rallied
in the great hall and were helplessly penned in as
soon as the massive doors were shut and braced on
the outside.

"Rats in a trap!" said Ben o' Coventry, as he
forced down a thick plank to hold a door. "We
need not slay one of them."

"I would I knew how it fareth with the
prince," said Richard. "Light every lamp and
beacon. I will go to the portal."

Prince Edward and they who were with him
were men certain to give a good account of themselves, but they had been none too many. The
warders at the town-wall gate had been small hindrance. The moment the huge oaken wings swung
back upon their hinges, up went the portcullis, out
shot the bridge across the deep, black moat, and
the blast of Sir Henry's horn was answered by the
rapid thud of hoofs as the prince led on his men-
at-arms.

"Straight for the middle square!" he shouted.
"Onward to the keep!"

"It is ours if Richard Neville be still living,"

calmly returned the knight. "Hark! the shouts
—the uproar!"

"Sir Thomas Gifford," commanded the prince,
"go to him. Take ten men-at-arms. We must
win the keep!"

On then he led his gallant men along the
street, but when they reached the central square
the French also were pouring into it from all
sides. Save for their utter surprise they would
have made a better fight, but at the first onset the
English lances scattered their hasty array like
chaff. Horsemen they had almost none, and their
knights who fought on foot were but half-armored.

Now also David Griffith and his Welshmen
had arrived within the walls, and it seemed to the
defenders of Bruyerre that their foemen were a
multitude. A band of mercenaries from Alsace,
three hundred strong, penned in a side street, surrendered without a blow at the first whizzing of
the English arrows.

Sir Thomas Gifford was standing at the portal
of the castle, and he saw a man in armor come hastily out into a light that shone beyond.

"Richard Neville," he asked, "how is it with
thee? Art thou beaten?"

"The keep is ours," called back Richard; "but
I have too many prisoners. There were six hundred men."

"St. George for England!" cried the astonished knight. "Thou hast done a noble deed of arms!"

"But Raoul de Bruyerre is dead, and so is Giles Monson, he who guided us," continued Richard. "How fareth the prince?"

"Go thou to him with thy good news," replied Sir Thomas. "I will take command here and finish thy work."

"Let us not remain with Sir Thomas," exclaimed the O'Rourke, behind Richard, "if there is to be more fighting."

"Nay, thou and thy kerns are garrison of the keep," said Sir Thomas.

So the hot-headed Irish chieftain had to bide behind stone walls to his great chagrin, while Richard went out gladly, with but a small party, to hunt for the prince through the shadowy, tumultuous streets of the half-mad town of Bruyerre.

There were faces at window crevices, and there were men and women in half-opened doorways. Richard continually announced to them, as had been the general order of the prince:

"In! In! Quarter to all who keep their houses, and death to all who come out!"

Brave as might be the burghers of Bruyerre, not many of those who heard cared to rush out alone, to be speared or cut down.

Before this, nevertheless, enough had gathered

at one point to feel some courage; and into this band Richard was compelled to charge.

With him were barely a dozen axemen and bowmen, yet he shouted in Norman French, as if to some larger force behind:

"Onward, men of Kent.! forward quickly! Bid the Irish hasten! St. George for England! For the king!"

The burghers had no captain, and they hardly knew their own number in the gloom. 'Twas a hot rush of desperate men against those who were irresolute. The burghers broke and fled to their houses, and on went Richard, having lost only a few of his small force.

The garrison had rallied faster and faster, and now almost surrounded in the square were the prince and his knights. Little they cared. Indeed, Sir Henry of Wakeham had said:

"What do you advise, my Lord Prince? We might even cut our way back to the castle, if we were sure of it. If we have that, we have command of the town."

"Hold your own here," replied the prince; "I think they give way somewhat."

Just then a band of bowmen, who had cleared out a side street, came forth as Richard went by.

"With me!" he called to them. "Let us join the prince. Beware how ye send your shafts into yonder *mêlée*, lest ye harm a friend!"

"Hark!" exclaimed Sir Henry. "It is Richard Neville! They have beaten him. Where can
Sir Thomas be? I fear there is black tidings!"

"Fight on!" replied the prince. "At all events
he bringeth us some help."

Closely aimed arrows, well-thrown spears, cleaving of sword and axe were help indeed; but better than all was the clear, ringing voice of Richard,
in English first, and then in Norman French:

"My Lord the Prince, we have the keep and
castle! Sir Thomas Gifford holdeth it. De Bruyerre is killed. His men are dead or taken. Bid
these fools here surrender. They have naught for
which to fight."

"God and St. George for England!" roared
Sir Henry of Wakeham.

"Hail to thee, Richard Neville!" sang out the
prince. "Victory! The town is ours! Bruyerre
is taken!"

All the Frenchmen heard, as well as all the
English. What was joy to one party was utter
discouragement to the other.

"Surrender!" commanded the prince. "The
fool who fighteth now hath his blood upon his
own head!"

Spears were lowered, swords were sheathed,
crossbows were dropped, brave men-at-arms gave
their names to Sir Henry and his knights, and the
peril in the great square was over.

"Well for us," coolly remarked Sir Henry. "The guards from the ramparts were arriving. My Lord of Cluse did not rightly number the garrison."

Nor had the English believed that so many townsmen could turn out so speedily. Nevertheless, when arms were given up the Frenchmen were no longer soldiers, and their numbers were of no more value.

"Richard Neville, I will well commend thee to my father! I think he will give thee thy spurs."

So spake the prince, with his hands on the shoulders of his friend, and looking into his face admiringly.

"Prince Edward," broke out the heir of Wartmont warmly, "I have done little. The taking of Bruyerre is thine. It was all thy plan."

"Mine? Nay," said the prince. "The best of it was prepared by Raoul de Bruyerre, when he held Giles Monson wickedly, that now an Englishman might be ready to let us in. So did his evil deed come back to his ruin."

"Aye," said Sir Henry; "but the dawn is in the sky, and the troops must be stationed fast. We will not stay to sack the town; but there are stores to gather, and there are knights of high degree to put to ransom. We have work to do."

So, quickly and wisely, went out the commands of the English captains, and the prize was made secure before the sun was an hour high.

13

Bitter enough was then the shame and wrath of knights and nobles of the garrison, as they learned by how small a force their great strong-hold had been surprised and taken. It should have been held for a year, they said, against all the army of King Edward.

All that bright summer day the business of sending away the garrison and of securing the best plunder of Bruyerre went industriously forward; but it was not in the hands of the Black Prince. Hardly had he finished eating a good repast in the castle, after having had courteous speech with Madame of Bruyerre and her household, before he gave command:

"Sir Robert Clifton, I appoint thee to the care of this place until I send thee orders from the king. He is now twelve miles away, and I must give him a report of this affair. Sir Henry and Gifford and Neville will go with me."

It was to horse and mount, then, while Robert Clifton cared for Bruyerre. The sun was looking down upon the midday halting of King Edward's own division of his army, when his son and his companions stood before him to tell him what they had done, and how.

Close and searching, as became a good general, were the questions of the king; but when all was done Sir Henry of Wakeham spoke boldly:

"Sire, is it not to be said that thy son and

Richard Neville have in this feat of arms well earned their spurs and chain of knighthood?"

"Truly!" came low but earnestly from Richard's uncle, the Earl of Warwick.

There was no smile upon the firm lips of the king, whatever his proud eyes might seem to say, and he replied:

"Not so, my good companion in arms. Think of thine own battles, many and hard fought. It were not well to forward them too fast. Neither my Edward nor Richard of Wartmont shall wear spurs until they have stood the brunt of one great passage of arms. Leave but a fair garrison in Bruyerre, for none will trouble them. We will march on to seek the field where we may meet the host of Philip of Valois. Word hath arrived that he is coming with all haste."

Forward, therefore, moved the forces of the king, and with them rode the two young companions in arms as simple squires; but the mighty field whereon they were to win their spurs was only a few days in the future.

CHAPTER IX.

GREAT had been the turmoil, the separation of comrades and of detachments, at the taking of Bruyerre. Hardly had Richard spoken twice to Sir Thomas Holland or Sir Peter Legh. Now, however, that the army of the king was once more moving forward, there was chance for them to ride together. Not until then, indeed, did it come clearly to Richard's mind how highly men thought of him for the taking and holding of the keep. Also, Sir Henry Wakeham had praised him much for his conduct in the perilous scaling of the walls by Giles Monson's secret pathway.

"I am well pleased," said Sir Peter, "that the order of march putteth thee and thy outlaws with Sir Thomas and me. So they take not us for deer and make targets of us, we are likely to render a good report to the king."

"Aye," added Sir Thomas dryly, "I knew not why even thy wild Irish kerns and thy Welsh savages took thee, more than another, for their chief-

188

tain, but I learned that they were like thy bow-men. Every man of them hath had a price set upon his head, for his good deeds before he was pardoned into the army."

"The king's deer will be safer after this cam-paign," said Sir Peter, "if, indeed, he is marching this army to meet the host of France. But that I trust him well, I would deem him safer on the other side of the Seine."

Now any who knew the province of Normandy and the parts that they were in, could see that the river Seine ran at the left of their march. It was between them and any seeming road to the taking of Calais. Well up the stream, in the direction they were taking, was the good city of Paris, with many strong forts, although it had no encircling wall. It lay open, with castles and fortified posts outside of its streets and palaces. At Paris, even now, there was a strong force of French, said to be equal in numbers to the English army. More forces were fast marching thitherward, but still King Edward was pushing on, as if he expected to capture the French capital by a swift dash and a surprise.

This was therefore the meaning of Sir Peter Legh, and it had been in the thoughts of many other men.

"Word hath come by many of the king's scouts," replied Richard, "that every bridge over the Seine hath been broken down by the French themselves, so that our army can by no means reach the other bank."

"Sir Thomas Holland," asked Sir Peter, "knowest thou what saith the king to that?"

"Nay," said Sir Thomas bluntly, "but I heard one Geoffrey of Harcourt, when a spy rode to him to tell that the last Seine bridge was down."

"What answered he?" asked Sir Peter.

"'Now all the saints be praised!' he said," responded Sir Peter. "'Philip of Valois doeth our business well. Their bridges are gone, and they can throw no force across the river to annoy our flank or rear. We have but a holiday march, unmolested."

Richard listened, that he might gather a lesson of war; but he said to the knights:

"I do but bethink me of what was said by one of my own men when he heard concerning the bridges. He is a carpenter from Coventry."

"What said he?" asked a deep voice behind them, as it were eagerly.

Then turned they all in their saddles, for there rode Sir Geoffrey of Harcourt, and with him was the prince.

"My Lord Marshal," said Richard, "he did but laugh, and he laughed loudly. Then he told his mates: 'Ye are but fools, and the king is wise. Give me our forest men and the two companies of

Kent and the London pikemen that are from the shipbuilding wards of London town. Then, if so be the king wanteth a bridge he can have one. We will even shape it in the woods in the morn, and have it over the stream at sunset.'"

"Richard Neville," said the marshal, "keep thou that saying to thyself, but search out thy man. Bid him and his to pick their wood workers, man by man. We shall have tools in plenty. The men do know each other. I was even now troubled in mind concerning handicraftsmen."

"No need, my Lord Marshal," reverently responded Richard. "I did hear more, and I can bring thee men that have built bridges over bigger streams than these."

"Richard of Wartmont," now broke in the prince, "ride thou with me a space. I would know more of thy men."

Then rode they silently until well apart from the others, and the prince said to his friend:

"This concerning the bridges will please the king. He hath said to me, of the commons and of thy Saxon kin, that now he hath a power that will grow fast, as he will help it grow. It hath not heretofore come to the hand of any king of England, and so some of them have been even too hardly dealt with by the great earls."

"I and mine are the king's men," said Richard, "and the king's only. But I learn many new things of war. It is more than hard fighting. But the King of France will have a great host."

"Oh that it were twice as great!" exclaimed the prince. "If my father can but gather it all, and as many more, at Paris, he will surely take Calais."

Richard could but laugh, and he replied:

"Far be it from me to read beforehand the counsel of so great a captain. I think that even when all is done, and he hath won his will, there will be those who will say that he never thought to do so."

"It is so ever," said the prince, "and therefore all the more surely doth he win. But I think any man might read beforehand the plan of this campaign. Only that none expected so much aid from Philip in this matter of the bridges."

There is both pleasure and profit to be had in discerning well the doings of the great, whereby battles are won or lost, and whereby thrones are builded or are overturned. Richard thought within himself that day and other days: "I do grow older as we march, and men have often said that war is a great school for such as will be taught. There be those who learn not anything. I will not be one of them."

On pressed the army, plundering as it went, and great spoil went back to England, but in its division the king cared for the lowly as well as for

the great, and there was no murmuring or dissatis-
faction among the men in the ranks.

Again and again was the river Seine approached
by the detachments of the left wing. Truly, every
bridge had been broken with care, to prevent a
crossing of the English. Richard had also many
talks with Ben of Coventry and with men who
were brought by him. These also were presented,
a dozen at a time, to Sir Geoffrey and the Earl of
Warwick, for the two marshals were of one accord
in this matter. No tools were dealt out, however,
nor was any work set the workmen, until a day
when the vanguard halted at a place called Poissy.
There was no French army here to meet them, and
yet the city of Paris itself was but a few miles farther on.

It was a gay sight, the lances and the pennons
that rode out with the van. Next came the royal
standard, and under it, in full armor and with
his crowned helmet on, full knightly rode the
king.

"Poissy!" he said. "Their last bridge, and it
shall be for me, although they have broken it
down. Where is that London shipwright? Ha,
man, look yonder! What sayest thou?"

A short man, sturdy of build, was the shipwright, for he had already been brought.

"My Lord the King," he responded, "I did go
on with the young Neville and that man of his

from Coventry. The bridge is good enough. The French took off the planks and some timbers, but they forgot to burn."

"Where are the timbers?" asked the king.

"Little on this side the river, but much on the other," said the shipwright. "All that is lacking we can make from these trees."

"Time!" exclaimed the king. "I must have the bridge forthwith! To your axes!"

"Boats first," said the shipwright. "There be many on the far bank."

"Sire," interposed the Earl of Warwick, "I pray thee have patience. Richard of Wartmont hath sent word to me concerning boats. I shall hear again shortly."

"See that he fail not," said the king hardly, for ever did his temper grow stern and unmerciful in such an hour as was this.

The army had now been led to the very place where all the plan of the king was to be tested, for winning or for losing, and here, mayhap, might his life or his crown be cast away.

Barely an hour earlier, however, lower down the river side, Richard Neville and a party of his men had been scouting, by command of Sir Thomas Holland. With him was the O'Rourke, and it was the Irish chief whose keen eyes were the first to discern an important prize.

"Richard of Wartmont," he shouted, "Seest

thou? Boats on the other shore! They are not even guarded."

"I could not swim this water," replied Richard. "Can any of them?"

"Aye," were it thrice—ten times as wide," said the O'Rourke. "I myself."

"Off with thy armor and axe!" cried Richard. "Call thy best swimmers. Bring me those boats. Guy the Bow, send a good runner to Sir Thomas Holland or Sir Peter Legh. Bid them, from me, to tell the earl or Sir Geoffrey I want a force to hold with on the other shore."

. Before he had finished speaking, the Irish chief and a dozen of his kerns were in the flood, swimming as if they had been so many water fowl; but each man's long skein dagger knife was in his belt, and in his left hand was a short spear, like those of the Welsh. They would not land unarmed.

"God speed them!" shouted Richard. "At no place heretofore have we seen a boat that we might hope to obtain."

'Twas a swiftly running river, and too wide for any but such swimmers as were these; but they made light of it. Ere they could cross, their coming was seen by men on the other shore, but none who were armed met them as they came out of the water. Surely it had been grave negligence of King Philip's officers to leave there so many as four fishing boats, even if these were small. Wild and shrill rang out the slogan of the Irish, as they seized upon oars and paddles and prepared to launch their prizes.

"They are out of arrow shot," said Richard to those who were with him; "we could give them no aid."

Even as he spoke, the glint of spears might be seen above bushes at no great distance down the opposite bank. No doubt there were horsemen coming. The Irish had been unwise to shout, but boat after boat was slipping into the stream.

"Haste! haste!" groaned Richard, "they will be lost, and the boats with them!"

A score of lances in rest—a score of galloping horses—loud shouts of angry men-at-arms—one moment of deadly peril—but then the brave kerns with the last of the boats were springing into it, and the French riders drew rein at the water's edge under a shower of javelins, only to know that they were too late.

It was just then, moreover, that Sir Thomas Holland, having listened eagerly to a Longwood archer, was shouting loudly, "To horse, brave knights all! The Neville hath found boats!" and orders followed to all foot soldiery within call.

"They come," said Richard, waiting his gallant kerns, "but yonder boats will hold only eight men each, well crowded. We can gain no land-

ing against men-at-arms. Yonder, above, is a
steeper bank, where horsemen can not reach the
brink—O'Rourke, on! Up stream!"

It was not far to go, and the French lancers
could do no more than follow as best they might,
over rough ground and through dense under-
growth. They were even out of sight, by reason
of the clifflike bank, when Richard Neville and
some of his bowmen made the boats full almost
to sinking, and were swiftly ferried over.

"Haste now, indeed!" he ordered, but not
loudly, as he stepped ashore. "A few boat loads
more and we can hold our own."

Whoever commanded the Frenchmen believed
his enemies to be going on up the river, for he
and his appeared on the bank again a full half
mile above. Again and again had the wherries
borne their English passengers, and now they were
going back for Sir Thomas Holland and the
knights who dismounted with him.

"Is the Neville mad?" he exclaimed. "He is
forming his archery on the hill. Look! 'Tis not
ill done. There come King Philip's men-at-arms!
Heaven help him! We are too late!"

"But the boy is not mad at all," replied Sir
Peter Legh. "The French horses go down. There
are not enough of them."

On the height, truly, had Richard formed his
threescore or more of kerns and bowmen, with

others fast arriving, but it was behind a thick, low hedge of old thorn bushes, fit to break a rush of cavalry. Here, therefore, was shattered the line of the French men-at-arms; and while they strove to force their horses through the thorns, they were good marks for the arrows of Arden. Their horses were but lost animals, and the good knights who rolled upon the ground surrendered rather than have Irish spears driven between the bars of their helmets. So rapid, so deadly was this killing of horses that not one did get away.

"I told thee!" said Sir Peter to Sir Thomas, in the boat that bore them. "We shall find that he hath done a brave deed this day."

More loudly did they both aver that thing when they came to the scene of the skirmish.

"Knights of ransom!" exclaimed Sir Thomas. "Did any escape?"

"I know not," said Richard, "but if more boats be at hand, above or below, they are to be sought for. May not these four ply here, while we march up the stream?"

"No use to scout below," replied Sir Thomas. "We are now twenty men-at-arms, on foot, and near a hundred of thy kerns and bowmen. March! We may all die, but we may win the bridge head."

On the other bank they could see the columns of Earl Warwick's men, sent hurriedly to re-enforce them, and shortly the O'Rourke shouted, "Another boat, and yet another twice larger, at the bank."

"That may save us," said Sir Peter, "but I would we were more in number."

So said the king himself, as he sat upon his palfrey and gazed across the Seine, not long thereafter. The French had not left the bridge without a guard, even if they had broken it down. Men of all arms were there, with many crossbowmen, and at first they had but laughed and derided what they supposed to be the utter disappointment of King Edward.

"Sire," exclaimed Sir Geoffrey of Harcourt, "the earl is right! Yonder are Richard of Wartmont and his men."

"Too few! Too few!" muttered the king. "He is over rash. He hath lost all."

All had been lost, indeed, but for the swift plying of the larger boats and the manner of their packing with brave men.

Sir Thomas Holland had now been joined by Gifford and Wakeham and good swords not a few, and the archers had swarmed into all boats like bees; with them were their stings, moreover, and most of all, mayhap, they came upon the French at the bridge as a surprise.

Loudly were they jeering, and the crossbowmen were even hurling a few useless bolts that fell halfway, as if to show the king what error he had made. There were many unarmed also, that crowded closely, mocking at the English.

Not upon these, but upon spearmen and cross-bowmen, there suddenly fell a flight of cloth-yard shafts, doing deadly work. In a moment the un-armed mob was tangled with the soldiery, and all these were in confusion. How many English were coming they knew not, for Sir Henry of Wake-ham had cunningly stretched out his line full widely, and it looked like a strong force. There were a few good French knights who set their spears in rest and charged rashly, to be unhorsed and taken, but the mixed mass behind them surged away from the bridge head. Here, too, had been a fort, not strong, but good enough for an occa-sion, and it was not at all broken.

"Richard Neville," had said Sir Peter, "follow me. If we can gain yonder tower and those pali-sades, the bridge is won."

Who would have deemed that a man in armor of proof could run so well! But Sir Peter was even shoulder to shoulder with Guy the Bow and Richard when they rushed into the empty fort-alice.

"Won!" shouted Sir Peter. "Let in our own, but the French will rally; they will be back upon us quickly enough."

Sir Henry and the rest had a sharp fight of many minutes ere they could break through, but

now the place was garrisoned, and the boats could
come in safety to the wharf below, behind the line
of palisades.

"Sire," said Sir Geoffrey, "I will myself go
over and care for the matter."

"Thou wilt not," replied the king. "I will
not risk thy head in that cage until more men-at-
arms may be with thee. There! 'tis Sir Henry of
Wakeham's own banner! I knew it not. The boy
and his outlaws have gained our crossing. Go, Sir
Geoffrey, and take with thee the bridge-builders."

It was well for him and them, nevertheless,
that their headlong rashness had not cost them
their lives, as it would have done, but for the
promptness and power of their re-enforcements.

"Wakeham," said Sir Geoffrey, in the bridge-
head fort, "I may hardly trust my eyes. Here
could Philip have given us vast trouble, and now
we have none. We will have a camp here quickly,
with ten thousand men in it, lest we lose this advantage."

There were boats enough now, and the forces
on that bank were growing fast. They were pushing out, moreover, and they were skirmishing
briskly with sundry parties of the enemy who
seemed to be without a general. Therein was the
secret of this matter. Philip of France had been
taken unawares by the bold, swift dash of Edward's army. Its vanguard had reached Poissy,

14

mayhap, two days before the French captains had deemed it possible for it to get there.

The night came and went, and it was the next midday when Richard Neville stood on the wharf, watching the London shipwrights ply their tools and swing the timbers into place.

"A man who would move an army," he said aloud, "must needs learn how to build a bridge. I can row a boat, but I must swim better. Those Irish are as nimble as fishes in the water."

A deep voice hailed him at the moment, and he quickly turned.

"Sir Geoffrey!" he exclaimed.

"This to the king," said the marshal, holding out a very small parcel, like a letter. "Come thou not back, save by the king's command, till thou hast carried this also to the earl. Take with thee only a boat load of thy men, but go not alone, for thy errand must not miscarry."

So happened it, then, that only David Griffith and a dozen Welshmen went with him, whose tongue he spoke not; but on the other shore his boat was waited for by the Earl of Warwick and none other, by chance.

"Glad am I," said Richard, giving him Sir Geoffrey's parcel, and the earl read hastily.

"To the king!" he shouted. "I go with thee. The good knight reasons well. We must harry and burn to the Paris streets, that we may know what power is there. He hath word that the allies and the levies of Philip of France are very near to come."

"The bridge buildeth fast," said Richard. " Ben of Coventry saith that by the morrow there will be a footway for twain abreast."

"Aye," replied the earl, "but not for horses nor for wains. Three days more for them."

The English army was now holding both sides of the stream, and the quarters of the king were in the old chateau of Poissy, not far from the bridge. Small was his care for state, however, and plain was his ordering, as of a soldier in the field. None hindered the earl marshal, and the king's officer of the house, that day, was Sir John of Chandos, good knight and true.

A greeting, a courteous reverence from Sir John to the earl, a word or so of command, and Richard was before the king in the audience hall of the chateau.

Cold, hard, and stern, like iron and like ice, was the face of his Majesty, as he opened and read the letter from Sir Geoffrey.

"Neville," said he to Richard, "hast thou spoken to any but the earl?"

"Not so, Sire," said Richard. "I did meet him at the river bank."

"Thou art young," said the king; "be prudent also, on thy head. Tell no man, high or low, that

Philip hath already forty thousand men in Paris. If thou shalt betray that matter, thou diest."

"He useth not his tongue overmuch," said the earl, for the king's word pleased him not. "But he hath somewhat more to say."

"Let him say on," growled the king, for it was shown that he was sore wroth ere they came.

"If it please the King," said Richard boldly, "a peasant whom I saw not fled from the city and had speech with some of the Welshmen. He was of Brittany, and their language was like to their understanding of each other. He saith not forty thousand, but less than half, only that they are mostly men-at-arms, with few horses to ride upon. There be many foot soldiers from Brittany. I would go around the city in one night, if David Griffith and another might go with me. Do not I speak French as do those I am to meet?"

"Wilt thou let him go, Warwick?" said the king. "It were death if he were taken."

"Richard, go thou!" said the earl. "If any question thee, tell that thou art Richard de la Saye, for I now give thee that estate of mine in Brittany. Thou wilt not speak falsely.—Sire, hath he not earned La Saye?"

"Verily, if he keep his head and bring back true tidings, he will have earned a manor or so," said the king less hardly. "I were in better mood with better news, but I have word from York. The archbishop is calling out all forces, for the Scottish clans are mustering and their host will march for the border forthwith. Moreover, our barons are sluggards, and our own re-enforcements do not come. We must even beat the French with what we have. Not a man more than we landed with at La Hague."

"I will retire, then," said the earl. "I will send Richard speedily."

Out they did go, but Sir John of Chandos shook his head and looked ruefully at Richard.

"Heed him not!" said the earl. "Keep thy heart strong. Make thou the circuit of Paris and come again. It will be the easier because I shall this night attack with a strong force the suburb and castle of St. Germain, near the city."

Many other things he said, but Richard sent for David Griffith, and they talked long together. Two more of Griffith's clansmen were called in, and both agreed with no murmuring.

On foot, clad in full armor, with his helmet closed, armed with but sword and dagger, attended only by the three Welshmen, as if they were armed serving men, did Richard at the gloaming walk slowly along the St. Germain road. By another way, he knew, the earl marshal was at that hour pushing forward his force, but the sound of the combat had not yet begun.

"We shall soon reach an outpost of the foe," he was thinking, when in a shadowed hollow be-yond him he heard one speak in French:

"Who cometh, in the king's name?"

"Normandy, with a countersign."

"Advance, Normandy, with the sign."

"For Philip the King, Guienne!"

"And all is well, Guienne," replied the sentry.

There was a slight clank of armor, for the French outpost was but changing sentries, and the officer rode away.

"Now we know sign and countersign," said Richard, and he carefully instructed his companions.

Hardly had he done so before a glare of red light, not far to the right, told of hayricks set on fire by Warwick's men. There came sounds of trumpets also, and of shouting, for the attack had begun.

"Forward, now," said Richard ; "we are safe, if once within their lines."

Loud and angry was the summons of the French vidette, startled sorely.

"De la Saye, Normandy, with a countersign," responded Richard.

"Advance, De la Saye and Normandy, with a sign," replied the sentry.

"To Philip the King, Guienne," said Richard, "and I bid thee save thy neck. The English are charging in."

"The Count d'Ivry," began the sentry. "Cease thy chatter!" exclaimed Richard. "Go tell the count, from De la Saye, that Earl Warwick is upon him. Bid him, from me, to send word speedily to the king, lest he lose his head."

"Aye, Sieur de la Saye," spoke yet another voice from one who sat upon a horse in the road. "Thou hast scouted far and well. I am the Count de la Torre, of Provence. I will report well of thee to the king. Our other scouts are worthless. What force sawest thou with the earl?"

"A thousand men-at-arms, about three thousand foot, in the advance. What more behind them knoweth no man. But there surely is no need to lose St. Germain this night."

Fiercely loud were the sayings of the count concerning the carelessness and bad management of the French captains. They had lost the bridge of Poissy. They were keeping but poor guard else-where. Now, but for this Sieur de la Saye, of Brittany, naught would have been known of War-wick's dash upon the city.

Therefore forward marched Richard and his Welshmen, and for a distance De la Torre rode beside them, questioning right soldierly concerning all that they had seen. But he spoke not, he said, the tongue of the peasants of Brittany.

"Were we all born in Paris," said David, after the count left him, " we could hardly be safer than we now are. But our peril will come in getting out."

"Great will it be," said Richard, "if we escape not before they change the countersign. We will walk fast and work while we may."

There were many camps to look upon, by their camp fires, and not too nearly. Richard himself had speech of even knights and men-at-arms, all of them disturbed in mind by the sudden advance of Earl Warwick. Each in turn, as it were, upbraided the slow arriving of King Philip's allies and levies, and especially of certain large bodies of mercenaries from the low countries and from Italy.

The Welshmen found no troops from Brittany until near the dawn, and then it was but at an outpost. Sleepy and dull were the half score of pikemen who were rudely aroused to hear the Sieur de la Saye scolding their brigadier for carelessness, and compelling him to repeat the countersign more correctly.

Griffith and his two men spake, and then they were silent, suddenly.

"On, my Lord of Wartmont!" whispered David hoarsely. "On, for thy head! Some of these men came from within two leagues of La Saye. One cometh to the brigadier."

A few quick paces and they were beyond the camp firelight. It was a place of trees and bushes. Sharp voices heard they contending and inquiring.

"Some one else hath come," said Richard. "The officer of the guard, with horsemen. Into the forest! Haste!"

Down dropped they behind cover, but men-at-arms went charging down the road, for one of the peasant pikemen had told to the brigadier, and then to a knight:

"The château La Saye is a heritage of the English Earl Warwick, and it hath no French owner."

"Go! a spy!" roared the knight. "We will teach him a lesson!"

A youth brought up near Longwood and three Welshmen from the hills were not men easily to be found in a forest; surely not by heavily armed French cavalry. It was high noon, nevertheless, when Richard marched wearily into an encampment over which floated the flag of Sir Thomas Gifford.

Free was his welcome; but when he stood before his good friend the knight he did but put a finger to his lips, and say:

"Sir Thomas, the king, and him only!"

"Speak thou no other word!" exclaimed Sir Thomas. "Come with me speedily. The earl

told me of thy going.   Glad am I to see thee again
alive."

No other was allowed to question them as they
went; but Sir Geoffrey of Harcourt, and not Earl
Warwick, was with King Edward when his young
spy of Paris stood before him.

"Speak thou slowly and with care," he said,
and Richard told his tale.

"Three days, and Philip's main host will be
within striking distance?" murmured the king at
last.   "Chandos, go thou to Warwick and bid
him smite fast and hard, burning tower and hamlet.
Harcourt, move every man and horse across the
bridge as fast as it will bear them.   Our five days
here will be enough for rest.   On the sixth we
must be a full day's march in advance of this huge
mob of French, Germans, Bohemians, Italians, and
what not.   Now, my lords and gentlemen, for a
great battlefield and for the taking of Calais.
Our barons of the north counties must deal with
David of Scotland and his overtreacherous raid."

Out went all orders speedily, but the prince,
with half the army, was already on the farther
bank of the Seine.   Richard's men were there also,
and he was sent to join them; but bitter and de-
structive was the work done by the earl marshal
in the outskirts of Paris, while the bridge was
finishing, and while the army moved on, out of
camp after camp.

Even as the king had commanded, the sixth day found his rear guard half a day's march beyond Poissy, seemingly in hot retreat. Philip of France had been as busy as had been his English rival, and his vast host was also moving. But it was not well in hand, nevertheless, for after that, from camp to camp, from river to river, day after day, the perfectly trained forces of Edward kept just beyond his reach, as if they were enticing him to follow.

There was many a sharp skirmish, and the French captains believed that their foe had often but narrowly escaped.

'Twas the king's plan, nor did he at any time hasten his march, and at last he said to his two marshals, mockingly:

"Philip hath me now, indeed, between his host and this river Somme and the sea. But I think the men and the beasts are not overwearied, and we have left but a desert behind us. Yet three days now, and we may need to retreat no more."

CHAPTER X.

"'Tis yet an hour before the tide will be out, but I believe that horsemen might cross now."

The speaker was a clownish-looking man wearing the wooden shoes and coarse blouse of a French peasant. He stood at the stirrup of a knight in black armor, whose questions he was answering.

"Sir Henry of Wakeham," the prince said, "send in thy men-at-arms. Post thy archers on the bank, right and left. We shall soon see if Godemar du Fay can bar the Somme against us."

"The archers are already posted," replied Sir Henry; "Neville and his Warwickshire men hold the right. The men of Suffolk and Kent are on the left."

"Forward, in the king's name!" commanded the young general, for his royal father had given him charge of the advance.

It was a critical moment, for if the ford of

212

Blanche Taque should not be forced, the entire English army would be hemmed in between the river Somme and the hosts of France. It was but little after sunrise, and Edward had sent orders to all his captains to move forward.

The river Somme was wider here than in its deeper channels above and below. The opposite bank was held by a force that was evidently strong, but its numbers were of less account at the outset. Only a few from either side could contend for the passage of Blanche Taque.

Therefore these were the chosen knights of all England who now rode into the water, finding it nearly up to their horse girths.

Forward from the other shore rode in the men-at-arms of Godemar du Fay to hold the ford for Philip of Valois.

"Now is our time!" shouted Richard to his archers. "Guy the Bow, let every archer draw his arrow to the head!"

Ill fared it then for the French riders when among them, aimed at horses rather than at men, flew the fatal messengers of the marksmen from the forest of Arden. Lances were fiercely thrust, maces and swords rang heavily upon helm and shield; but soon the French column fell into confusion. Its front rank failed of support and was driven steadily back. It was almost as if the English champions went on without pausing; and in a

few minutes they were pushing forward and widen-
ing their front upon the land.

Blanche Taque was taken, for of Godemar du
Fay's twelve thousand, only a thousand were men-
at-arms. When the regular ranks of these were
broken, his ill-disciplined infantry took to flight
and the battle was over. All the while the tide
was running out.

"Stand fast, O'Rourke!" called Richard to the
impatient Irish chieftain, who was striding angrily
back and forth in front of his line of axemen.

"Ay, but, my Lord of Wartmont," returned the
O'Rourke, "there is fighting, and we are not in the
battle. Hark!"

"Neville, advance! Thou and all thine to the
front, seeking Wakeham. In the king's name, forward!"

A knight in bright armor had drawn rein at a
little distance, and he pointed toward the ford as
he spoke. It was crowded still by Sir Thomas
Gifford's men-at-arms, but the battle on the other
shore had drifted far away.

"Forward, O'Rourke!" shouted Richard. "Forward, Guy the Bow! Forward, David Griffith!
Good fortune is with us. We are to be under the
prince's own command."

Loud cheers replied, and with much laughter
and full of courage Richard's force waded into the
shallow Somme.

It was easy crossing now for all, with none to hinder. Then, as the last flags of the English rear-guard fluttered upon the left bank of the Somme, good eyes might have discovered on the horizon the banners of the foremost horsemen of King Philip. He had marched fast and far that morning, and once more the English army seemed barely to have escaped him.

"A cunning hunter is our good lord the king," remarked Ben o' Coventry to his fellows as they pushed on.

"Thou art ever malapert," said Guy the Bow. "What knowest thou of the thoughts of thy betters?"

"He who runs may read," said Ben. "Can a Frenchman live without eating?"

"I trow not," responded Guy. "What is thy riddle?"

"Did we not waste the land as we came?" said Ben. "Hath not Philip these three days marched through the waste? I tell thee that when he is over the Somme he must fight or starve. Well for us, and thanks to the king, that we are to meet a host that is both footsore and half famished. I can put down a hungry man any day."

Deep indeed had been the wisdom of the king, and his army encamped that Thursday night, without fear of an attack, and the next morning they again went on.

Edward himself rode forward in the advance, after the noontide of Friday, and during the whole march he seemed to be searching the land with his eyes.

"Sir John of Chandos," he exclaimed at last, "see yon windmill on the hill. This is the place I sought. Ride thou with me." The hill was not very high, and its sides sloped away gently. The king dismounted at the door of the mill and gazed in all directions.

"They will come from the west," he said, "with the sun in their eyes. Yon is our battlefield. Here we will bide their onset. Chandos, knowest thou that I am to fight Philip of Valois on mine own land?"

"The village over there is called Crécy," replied Sir John. "Truly, the crown of France is thine, rather than Philip's!"

"Ay, so," said Edward, "whether or no he can keep it from me; but this broad vale and the village and the chateaux are my inheritance from my grandmother. Seest thou that ditch to the right, with its fellow on the left? I trust they have good depth. 'Tis a field prepared!"

After that he rode slowly, with his son and a gallant company, throughout the camps, talking kindly and familiarly with high and low alike, and bidding all to trust God and be sure of victory. Brave men were they, and well did they love their king, but it was good for their courage that they should see his face and hear his voice, and assure their hearts that they had a great captain for their commander.

In number they were about as many as had sailed at the first from England, small losses by the way, and the absence of those left as garrisons of strongholds captured in Normandy, having been made good by later arrivals.

This first duty done, the king went to his quarters in the neighboring castle of La Broye, and here he gave a grand entertainment to all his captains and gentlemen of note. There was much music at the royal feast, and every man was inspired to do his best on the morrow. All the instruments sounded together loudly, at the close, when the warriors, who were so soon to fight to the death, arose to their feet and stood then in silence, while the king and the prince turned away and walked out of the hall together, no man following.

" Whither go they ? " whispered the Earl of Hereford to Sir John Chandos.

" As it doth well become our king at this hour," replied Sir John. " They go to the chapel of La Broye to pray for victory. 'Twill do our men no harm to be told that the king and the prince are on their knees."

" Verily, my men shall know," said Richard Neville to Sir Thomas Gifford.

15

All of Edward's army, save the watchers and
sentries, slept soundly that night. It was wonder-
ful how little uncertainty they had about the result
of the battle.

The morning came, but there were clouds in the
sky and the air was sultry. It was Saturday, the
26th of August, 1346.

Edward the king posted himself at the windmill. On the slope and below it were a third of
his men-at-arms and a strong body of footmen.
This was the reserve. In front thereof, the remainder of the army was placed in the form of a
great harrow, with its point—a blunt one enough
—toward the hill, and its beams marked by the
ditch lines.

The right beam of this English harrow was
commanded by the Black Prince in person, and
with him were the Earls of Warwick and Hereford, Geoffrey of Harcourt, and Sir John Chandos,
with many another famous knight. Their force
was less than a thousand men-at-arms, with many
Irish and Welsh, but they were especially strong
in bowmen, for the king retained few archers
with him.

But little less was the strength of the left beam
of the harrow, commanded by the earls of Northampton and Arundel.

"Fortune hath favored us!" exclaimed one of
the men-at-arms to his young commander; " we

are well placed here at the right. We shall be among the first to face the French ! "

" Here cometh the prince," responded Richard, " with his Red Dragon banner of Wales. The royal standard is with the king at the mill."

Reviewing the lines with care, and giving many orders as he came, the prince rode up, clad in his plain black armor and wearing the helmet of a simple esquire.

" Richard Neville," he said, as he drew near, " see that thou dost thy devoir this day."

Richard's head bowed low as the prince wheeled away. As he again sat erect upon his war horse a voice near him muttered :

" Ho ! seest thou ? The French are coming ! "

Richard looked, and in the distance he could see a glittering and a flag, but after a long gaze he replied :

" It is too soon. Those are but a band of skir-mishers."

So it proved ; and the long, hot hours went slowly by. At length the king ordered that every man should be supplied with food and drink, that they might not fight fasting.

Darker grew the clouds until they hung low over all the sky. Blue flashes of lightning were followed by deafening thunder peals, and then there fell a deluge of warm rain.

The English archers were posted in the front

ranks along the harrow beams, but the rain harmed not their bows. Every bowstring was as yet in its case, with its hard spun silk securely dry.

"Hearken well, all," said Richard, addressing his men. "The prince ordereth that there shall be no shouting. Fight with shut lips, and send forth no shaft without a sure mark."

"We are to bite, and not to bark," said Ben o' Coventry in a low voice. Then he added aloud: "Yon marshy level is better for the rain. A horse might sink to his pasterns."

"The ditch runneth full," said Richard. "The king chose his battle ground wisely."

"We are put behind the archery now," said David Griffith to his Welshmen. "So are the Irish; but our time to fight will come soon enough."

Most of the men-at-arms belonging to each beam of the harrow were drawn up at the inner end, ready to mount and ride, but wasting no effort now of horse or man.

"The very rain hath fought for England," remarked the prince to his knights, as at the front they wheeled for their return. "There will be hard marching for the host of Philip of Valois."

"They must come through deep mud and tangled country, my Lord the Prince," replied the Earl of Warwick. "His huge rabble of horse and foot will be sore crowded and well wearied."

Moreover, there was much free speech among the knights concerning the difference between the opposing armies as to their training and discipline.

King Philip willed to begin the fight with an advance of his Genoese crossbowmen, fifteen thousand strong. It was bolts against arrows. The Genoese might have done better on another day, for their fame was great; but at this hour they were at the end of a forced march of six leagues, each man carrying his cumbrous weapon with its sheaf of bolts. This had weakened their muscles and diminished their ardor; besides, the sudden rain had soaked their bowstrings. The cords stretched when the strain of the winding winch was put upon them, and had lost their spring, so that they would not throw with good force. Their captains nevertheless drove them forward, at the French king's command.

From his post at the mill foot the royal general of England surveyed the field.

"The day waneth," he said to his earls, "but the waiting is over. The sun is low and sendeth the stronger glare into their eyes. Mark you how closely packed is that hedge of men-at-arms and lances behind the Genoese? Philip is mad!"

On pushed the crossbowmen, until they were well within the beams of the broad harrow, but there they halted, to do somewhat with their bolts, if they could; and they sent up a great shout. No answer came, for the English archers stood silent, holding each a cloth-yard arrow ready for the string.

Small harm was done by the feebly shot cross-bow bolts, and the Genoese were ordered to go nearer. They made a threatening rush indeed; but then of their own accord they halted again and shouted, thinking perhaps to terrify the English army.

Steady as statues stood the archers until the Earl of Hereford, at a word from the prince, rode out to where he could be seen by all and waved his truncheon.

Up came the bows along the serried lines, while each man chose his mark as if he were shooting for a prize upon a holiday in merry England.

Those of the enemy who escaped to tell the tale said afterward that then it seemed as if it snowed arrows, so swiftly twanged the strings and sped the white shafts.

With yells of terror the stricken Genoese broke and fled; for by reason of Edward's order of bat-tle they were in a cross fire from the two beams of the harrow, and few shots failed of a target among them.

Some of them even cut the damp strings of their useless crossbows as they went, lest they should be bidden to turn and fight again. They were now, however, only a pell-mell mob, and it was impossible to command them.

Behind the advance of the Genoese had been the splendid array of King Philip's men-at-arms—a forest of lances. In a fair field, and handled well, they were numerous enough to ride down the entire force of King Edward. Against such an attack the English king had cunningly provided. At no great distance in the rear of his knights rode Philip himself, with kings and princes for his company; and fierce was his wrath over the unexpected discomfiture of his luckless cross-bowmen.

"Slay me these cowardly scoundrels!" he shouted to his knights. "Charge through them, smiting as ye go!"

Forward rode the thousands of the chivalry of France and Germany and Bohemia, every mailed warrior among them being full of contempt for the thin barrier of English foot soldiers. All they now needed, it seemed to them, was to disentangle their panoplied war horses from that crowd of panic-stricken Genoese. It would also be well if they could pass the wet ground and avoid plunging against one another in the hurly burly.

But now was to be noted another proof of the wise forethought of the English king. He had had prepared, and the prince had placed at short intervals along the battle line, a number of the new machines called "bombards." These were short,

hollow tubes, made either of thick oaken staves,
bound together with strong straps of iron, or (as
was said of some of them) the staves themselves
were bars of iron. Before this day, none knew
exactly when, there had been discovered by the
alchemists a curious compound that, packed into
the bombards, would explode with force when
touched by fire, and hurl an iron ball to a great
distance. It would hurt whatever thing it might
alight upon; but the king's thought was rather
that the loud explosions and the flying missiles
might affright the mettled horses of the French
men-at-arms.

Soon the air was full of the roaring of these
bombards, and they served somewhat the king's
purpose. But so little was then thought of this
use of gunpowder at Crécy that some who chronicled
the battle, not having been there to see and hear,
failed even to mention it.

The fine array of the gallant knights was now
confused indeed. They vainly sought to restore
their broken order. Not only the manner of the
flight of the Genoese, and the greater force and
longer line of the right beam of the English harrow invited them to urge their steeds in that direction, but there also floated the Red Dragon banner
of the Prince of Wales. Well did each good
knight know that there was beating the heart of
the great battle.

Soon the air was full of the roaring.

Worse than the noisy wrath of bombards came now at the command of the prince. To right and left, plying their bows as they went, wheeled orderly sections of the archery lines, that through those gaps might pass the fierce rush of the wild Welshmen. They were ordered forward, not to contend with knights in armor of proof, but to slay the horses with their javelins.

Terrible was the work they did, darting lightly to and fro; and it was pitiful to see so many gallant knights rolled helplessly upon the ground, encumbered by their armor. Nevertheless, many kept their saddles, and broke through the Welsh to find themselves forced to draw rein in front of the deep ditches that guarded the archery, who were ever plying their deadly bows.

"Down lances!" shouted the Black Prince to his men-at-arms, at the head of the harrow. "For England! For the king! St. George! Charge!"

More than two thousand mailed horsemen, of England's best, struck their spurs deep as the royal trumpet sounded. Riders and horses were fresh and unwearied.

There was the thunder of many hoofs, a crash of splintering lances, and they were hand-to-hand with King Philip's disordered chivalry. Well for him and his if he had then sounded a recall, so that his shattered forces might be rearranged; but instead, he poured forward his reserves, thereby increasing the pressure and the tumult, while the English archers ever plied their bows with deadly effect.

It was then that the blind King of Bohemia, the ally of Philip in this war, was told how the day was going. At his side rode several of his nobles, and he said to them :

"I pray and beseech you that you lead me so far into the fight that I may strike one blow with this sword of mine."

He had been accounted a knight of worth in his youth, and the spirit of battle was yet strong upon him, neither did there yet seem to be good reason why his request should not be granted. Therefore his friends on either hand fastened the bridle bits of their horses on a line with his own, and they rode bravely forward together.

Right hard was the strife that now went on, especially between the beams of the harrow and toward the right. In the midst of it floated the Red Dragon flag, and here the prince and his companions in arms were contending against the greater numbers of their assailants. Here was the center toward which all were pressing, and here, it was seen, the fate of the battle was to be decided. For this very reason the pressure was less upon the left beam of the harrow, and its captains could the better observe the marvelous passage at arms around the prince.

"Sir Thomas Norwich," spoke the Earl of Northampton, " we must all go forward and do our best. Ride thou to the king, and crave of him that he send help with speed. We fear it is full time for the reserves to move, if it be not even now too late."

Then the Earl of Arundel and other knights lowered their lances, and setting spurs to their horses charged into the thickest press.

Away spurred the knight of Norwich, and ere many minutes had elapsed he gave the message to the king at the foot of the windmill; for there had the king been standing all the while watching the course of the battle with better perception than could be had by any of those who were in it. .He could therefore discern in what manner Philip of Valois was defeating himself, crushing his own forces.

" Is my son dead, or unhorsed, or so wounded that he can not help himself?" he calmly inquired of the messenger.

"No, Sire," responded Norwich; "but he is in a hard passage at arms, and sorely needeth your help."

"Return thou, Sir Thomas, to those who sent thee," said the king, "and bid them not to send to me so long as my son liveth. Let the boy win his spurs; for, if God so order it, I will that the day may be his, and that the honor may be with him and with them to whom I gave it in charge."

No more could the good knight say, and back he rode without company.

There were those who thought it hard of the king, but better it was that he should hold his reserves for utter need.

Nevertheless, the aspect seemed to be growing darker to the true English hearts that were fighting in the press. They saw not, as the king did, that, owing to his cunning plan of battle, more in number of the English than of the enemy were at any instant actually smiting, save at the center, around the prince himself.

Dark as was the seeming, the heart of none was failing.

" To the prince ! To the prince !" shouted Richard Neville, as the space in front of him was cleared somewhat of foemen. " Follow me !" Forward he went, and loudly rang out behind him the battle shouts of his men. They were fewer than at the beginning, but boldly and loyally they had closed up shoulder to shoulder.

Richard's horse was slain under him by a thrust from a German pike; but the rider was lifted to his feet in time to meet the rush of the King of Bohemia and his friends. Their horses were sadly hampered by that hitching together of bridles, and were rearing, plunging, unmanageable. More than one blow had the old, blind hero given that day, as he had willed. None knew now by whose arrows his horse and those of his comrades went down, but after they were unhorsed the wild tide of the battle passed over them, for none of them rose again.

"To the prince!" shouted Richard fiercely. "I saw his crest go down!"

The arrows and darts flew fast as the young hero of Wartmont fought his way in amid the crash of swords and lances.

"Now, Heaven be praised!" he cried out, "I see the prince! He liveth!"

He said no more, for before him stood a tall knight with a golden wing upon his helmet, and wielding a battle-axe.

Clang, clang, followed blow on blow between those twain. It had been harder for Richard but that his foe was wearied with the heat and the long combat. Well and valorously did each hold his own, but a blow from another blade fell upon Richard's bosom, cleaving his breastplate. Then, even as he sank, across him strode what seemed some giant, and a wild cry in the Irish tongue went up as the O'Rourke poleaxe fell upon the shoulder of the knight of the golden wing.

"On!" shouted the furious chief. "On, men of the fens! Forward, Connaught and Ulster!

Vengeance for our young lord! Down with the French?"

Hundreds of strong Irish had followed their leader, and timely indeed was their coming, for the sun was sinking, and need was to win the victory speedily.

"Alas!" said Guy the Bow, as he bent over Richard. "I pray thee, tell me, art thou deadly hurt, my lord?"

"Lift me!" gasped Richard. "Put me upon my feet. I would fight on and fall with the prince."

Quickly they lifted him, but he staggered faintly and leaned upon Guy the Bow.

"I fear he is sore hurt," muttered Guy.

But at that moment there arose a great shouting. It began among the reserves who were with the king on the slope of the hill.

"They fly! The foe are breaking! The day is ours! The field is won! God and St. George for England, and for the king!"

It was true, for the army of the King of France could bear no more. All things were against them. They could neither fight in ranks nor flee from the cloth-yard shafts.

The prince came near the group around Richard, and, pausing from giving swift orders to his knights, he stepped forward.

"'Tis Richard of Wartmont!" he exclaimed. "Is he dying?"

"Arise, Sir Richard of Wartmont!"

Straight up stood Richard, raising his visor. He was ghastly pale, but his voice had partly come back to him.

"I think not, Prince Edward," he faltered. "But I thank Heaven that thou art safe !"

"Courage !" said the prince. "The field is ours, and thou hast won honor this day. Bear him with me to the king."

Here and there brave fragments of what had been the mighty host of France held out and still fought on ; but they were not enough. All others sought to save themselves as best they might from the pitiless following of the English. Those in the rear who fled at once were safe enough, and the sunset and the evening shadows were good friends to many more of the French. Most fortunate were such horsemen as had not been able to get into the harrow, for only about twelve hundred knights were slain. With them, however, fell eleven princes and the King of Bohemia, and thirty thousand footmen. The King of France himself was a fugitive that night, seeking where he might hide his head.

From his place on the hill King Edward of England watched the closing of the great day of Crécy, and now before him stood a strange array. Shorn plumes, cloven crests or none, battered and bloody armor, broken swords, shivered lances, battle-worn faces, lighted somewhat by pride of victory, were arrayed before him. All were on foot, and each man bowed the knee.

Few, but weighty and noble with thanks and honor, were the words of the king. More he would say, he told them, when he should better know each man's meed of praise.

At length the Black Prince came forward, and he knelt before his father, to rise a knight; for he had won his spurs.

"Richard of Wartmont!" cheerily spoke the king. "Come thou!"

"Sore wounded, Sire," said Sir Henry of Wakeham; "but I will aid."

"Not so," exclaimed the prince. "I will bring him myself."

When Richard was brought before King Edward, he heard but faintly the words that made him a knight:

"Arise, Sir Richard of Wartmont!"

All strength and life that were yet in Richard had helped him to lean upon the prince's arm, to kneel, to rise again, and to hear, almost without hearing, the good words of the king. Then he stepped backward, and Guy the Bow put an arm around him and said lovingly:

"Sir Richard of Wartmont, proud will thy lady mother be! I trow the war is over. When thy wounds are well healed we will take thee home to her."

Long after the sun went down strong detachments of King Edward's army were busily at work
gathering in the fruits of the victory. Not that
there was any effort to take prisoners of the common men, but that many knights who could pay
good ransom lay upon the field sore wounded or
encumbered with their armor. Moreover, there
was great spoil of arms, and of other matters of
war and peace.

Heavily slumbered Richard Neville, and a careless watcher might have thought him dead; but
those who were with him watched lovingly, listening for every breath, and moving him with care at
times.

"He waketh!" whispered Guy the Bow, as the
light began to come in through the high window
of the room in the château La Broye. "The
leech will soon be here."

Even as he spoke there entered a small, slight
man in the black dress of the king's physicians. No
word he spoke, but he bent low over the sword
mark upon Richard's ribs, removing its cover.

"Is this all?" he asked of Guy.

"Save bruises," said Guy, "no other hurt have
we found."

"The youth will do well," replied the leech.
"He fell rather from heat and exhaustion of the
long fray than from this blow. Not a rib is cut
through."

16

He gave simple directions only, and he passed out, but he heard from Ben of Coventry :

"That man hath good sense. My Lady of Wartmont will not lose her son."

"But the leech did it not," said Guy. "More was done by the thickness of yonder cloven breast-plate. He will need long rest."

So did the army, but the king gave it no more than was needful. Before the close of that day all knew that the King of France himself had been taken, and that the war had no more great battles in it.

All news was brought to Richard by his friends, for among them came Earl Warwick and Sir Geoffrey and the Earl of Arundel, and many another whose coming was high honor to the young Knight of Wartmont.

Only the third day thence, and Richard stood almost firmly upon his feet, for Sir John Chandos entered the room.

"The king," he said, "and with him is the prince."

In a moment more it was to Richard as if he had gained sudden strength, for before him stood the two royal warriors.

"Nay, man, sit thee down !" commanded the king ; but the Black Prince stepped forward and grasped his hand.

"I heard thee, Richard Neville," he said most

graciously—"I heard thee in the fray, when thou didst bid thy men fight on and die with thee and me. I will trust thee!"

The king had looked kindly into Richard's face, and now he spoke again :

"Neville of Wartmont, whether or not thou goest to the seashore in a litter, thou wilt set out to-morrow. Haste is not needed so much as a trusty messenger. Thy packet will be ready for thee, and thou wilt also have in thy mind unwritten words for the Archbishop of York. Rest thou to-night. The prince will come to thee, not I; so will the earl."

Not long were ever the speeches of the king, but Sir John Chandos now came in again, for he had left them, and with him he brought a sword with a silver hilt and cross.

"This is for thee, Richard Neville," said the prince, "for thine own was broken. Wear it bravely thou wilt. It was found among the baggage of the King of France, and they say it hath been carried by more than one crowned head. It is my token of good will, and the king's."

Richard knelt low to take the sheathed blade, but as he arose they departed. A little later it was as if all the archers of Longwood felt that the royal sword had been given to them, so proud were they of their young knight and captain.

Full a hundred of them, moreover, were per-

mitted to return by ship with Richard. Much
spoil went with them, and more had gone before
them, and each man went with a promise and a
command to return with many men like himself
to aid the king before the walls of Calais.

Not in a litter would Richard travel the next
day, after long converse with the prince, but
upon an ambling palfrey whose paces pained
him not.

It was a small seaport to which the prince's
order sent him. Even three long days were
wasted before the arrival of the craft that was to
bear Richard and his men across the Channel.
Rough, not smooth, was their passage to Portsmouth, but the sea was clear of all foemen.

It was well on in September, therefore, when
a column of bowmen, with Richard at their head,
rode through the gate of Warwick town. The
tidings of Crécy had reached the whole land much
earlier, but the people poured out of all the houses
to see the first returning of the men who had won
the great day.

Richard now rode a good horse and wore his
armor, with the crested helmet of a knight, with a
gold chain and spurs, and he was girded with the
king's gift sword.

There was great shouting, and the Mayor met
him, bidding him to a feast at the Town Hall,
where many knights and gentlemen and rich

burghers were to welcome him, and to hear whatever he could tell of the war in France.

This, too, he well knew, was of the will of the
king, to stir the loyalty of his lieges at home and
to content them concerning the taxes he yet must
levy.

But on rode Richard to the castle gateway, and
therein were many noble women.

"I see her!" he thought. "Is she not beautiful in her long white robe and with the pearls in
her white hair?"

Down sprang the young knight, as if he had
had never a wound, but ere his feet were on the
earth his mother's arms were around him.

"I have thee again!" she exclaimed. "Thou
art like thy father, O my son!"

She was silent then, and her eyes were closed,
but her lips moved a little. If it were a prayer of
thanks, its words were heard only by Him who is
above.

The Countess of Warwick came next, and
many that were Nevilles or Beauchamps, or of
kindred houses, and they led him on into the
castle.

"Mother," he said, "it is almost like a
dream!"

"Thou wilt rest thee here," she said, after he
told under what duty he was bound. "I can not
let thee go at once."

"The king bade me make no haste," he replied, "but rather to be his newsman to all who would inquire of the army and of its deeds. So shall there be better content."

It was a grand feasting at the Town Hall. The archers from Crécy field were feasted by them-selves ere they set out for home, and many a stout bowman who saw how well they were and heard their tales, was eager to march with them when-ever the king again might send to bid them muster.

Of necessity the resting at Warwick was but brief, and then Sir Richard Neville and a party of men-at-arms rode northward. Not in haste, like his first journey, was this he was making now. Hard was it to pass by or to get away from any tower or town to which he came; but every-where he did the errand upon which the king had sent him, and everywhere were all men readier than before in their loyalty and their service of the crown, whether they were barons or commons.

Even more than to the king was the praise they were willing to give the prince.

Once again, as he drew near, did Richard won-der at the spire of York Cathedral, and once more was he led on into the audience hall, and then into the oratory of the archbishop, that he might deliver privately the letters and the messages of the king. Pale somewhat was the face of the good prelate, but very calmly he read and he listened.

"My son," he said at last, "all is well. We will give God praise for the good news from France, but thou knowest that the Scottish host is in England?"

"I have heard much," said Richard.

"Then know also that ere this they are face to face with our own lines. A battle as great as that of Crécy——"

Loud shouts were heard in the street without, and then in the great hall.

"My son!" exclaimed the archbishop, listening with lifted hand.

Open swung the door, and a barefooted friar rushed in.

"My Lord Archbishop! A knight from the battle! The Scottish host is defeated——"

But close behind him strode a man in armor, covered with dust, unhelmeted, and marked by a fresh sword cut on his face.

"I waited not, my Lord Archbishop," he said. "King David of Scotland is a prisoner! His army is routed! He hath lost his crown!—What, Richard, art thou here?"

"Praise be to Heaven, Sir Robert Johnstone!" responded the archbishop. "He cometh from the king's victory at Crécy——"

"Knighted!" exclaimed Sir Robert. "Then I will tell thee, Sir Richard Neville of Wartmont, this victory of our English bowmen over the clans and the men-at-arms of Scotland hath been won at the field of Neville's Cross. All the king's counsel hath prevailed, and his realm is safe!"

THE END.

www.ingramcontent.com/pod-product-compliance
Lightning Source LLC
Chambersburg PA
CBHW030132060726

47499CB00015B/1601